SMALL MOMENTS

ILLINOIS SHORT FICTION

Other titles in the series:

Rolling All the Time by James Ballard

Love in the Winter by Daniel Curley

To Byzantium by Andrew Fetler

Crossings by Stephen Minot

A Season for Unnatural Causes by Phillip F. O'Connor

Curving Road by John Stewart

Such Waltzing Was Not Easy by Gordon Weaver

SMALL MOMENTS

Stories by

Nancy Huddleston Packer

UNIVERSITY OF ILLINOIS PRESS

Urbana Chicago London

Manufactured in the United States of America

"Early Morning, Lonely Ride," *Southwest Review*, LII, 4 (1967)
"Night Guard," *The Kenyon Review*, XXIII, 1 (1961)
"Oh Jerusalem," *Contact*, III, 1 (1961)
"Second Wind," *Southwest Review*, LVIII, 3 (1973)
"Once a Thief . . ." *Southwest Review*, XLVIII, 3 (1963)
"Front Man in Line," *The Yale Review*, LV, 1 (1965)
"Shadow of an Eagle," *The Kenyon Review*, XXV, 2 (1963)
"End of a Game," *Ararat*, VIII, 4 (1967)
"We Two—Again," *Barataria Review*, I, 1 (1975)
"One of These Days . . ." *The Kenyon Review*, XXII, 2 (1960)
"Martin Fincher, Tripod Man," *Stanford Short Stories*, 1960, ed. Wallace Stegner and Richard Scowcroft (Stanford University Press)

Library of Congress Cataloging in Publication Data

Packer, Nancy Huddleston.
Small moments.

(Illinois short fiction)
CONTENTS: Early morning, lonely ride.—Night guard.—Oh Jerusalem.—Second wind. [etc.]
I. Title.
PZ4.P1185Sm [PS3566.A318) 813'.5'4 76-7601
ISBN 0-252-00615-1
ISBN 0-252-00616-X pbk.

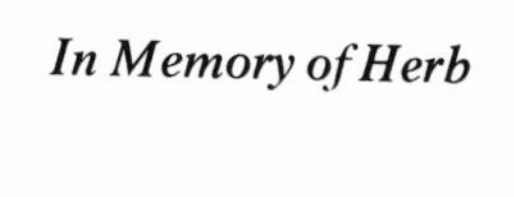
In Memory of Herb

Contents

Early Morning, Lonely Ride

Frances Benedict's husband, Emery, was a lawyer. Successful. Frances herself might yet become anything, having tried nothing. She was only thirty-three. She had three children and live-in help at home. Sleeping. She was nothing among strangers at a rich man's party. She said to Emery, "Notice how new money smells like a cross between wet copper and Cashmere Bouquet?"

"Please don't," said Emery.

"Cash, cashmere, coppers, copper, and a can of room freshener I think they call it wafting in from the downstairs drains. Rich people always trying to undo the natural odors of the universe. New rich. What about dying? Buried with a can of aerosol spray and a couple of lavender sachets?" She thought she was going just great, about to zoom off holding Emery by the collar.

"Grow up," said Emery, making his choice against her. "Please just grow up!"

"Right here?" she asked sweetly. "On his gorgeous handwoven rug? Think of the aroma for God's sake, Emery."

Gazing beyond her with the look of a guest who expects momentarily to catch the party's beat, Emery professed to ignore her, having other fish to fry or why had they come in the first place. To cope with her, she believed, required his full attention. Hell with it. She sat on a pumpkin velvet window seat and vowed to view the dark bay all evening. Maybe the rich didn't like smells but they sure bought the sights. If anyone noticed. Occasionally she nodded amiably about her. Grins hung from her teeth like old moss. People seeing her saw only Revlon and Maidenform. She was just one of the girls, boys: chic, shrewd, and stupid. Look out. Their hostess, whose barbiturated face flamed up from a purple dress that weighed in at close to five hundred dollars, claimed Emery, rescued a man from his wife. From time to time, the host, porpoise of body but ferret of eye, came to sit beside Frances and to press thighs with her. Frances shortly ran out of amusing things to say and was a wallflower. With contemptuous lack of embarrassment she warded off other wallflowers seeking solace. She was not a woman's woman. With a cold blue mirthless eye she forewarned idle men she might have ridden straight through the evening. She was not a man's woman.

It was Emery's crowd, not hers. It was a tired coupling of business and pleasure. She did not count. She was, if anything at all, only a helpmeet the color of the background. Forgetting her, Emery enjoyed himself. At that thought, many grievances surfaced. The children slept like tops; like tops they were spinning on their own. Strings dangled from her hands, cut loose by time and condition. Nothing short of the rapt attention of everyone would satisfy her and, sadly, she knew it. She grew restive. This was the world she lived in, a world she never made, the best of all possible worlds, but hers, alas, was not the hand that rocked it.

"O brave new world," she said aloud.

"Darling?" asked Emery, standing at the empty fireplace with their host's brother-in-law, for all the world as if conducting the world's affairs.

"That has such people in it," she finished.

Emery laughed gaily, apprehensively, and moved away. The brother-in-law, who smelled of oil and litigation and pine needles, cast her an appraising and impersonal look. The sort of man, she decided, who grandly bestowed upon a grateful wife a white Lincoln Continental. (What's wrong with that? Emery might ask. If you don't know . . . Did *she* give *him* a Cadillac?) Frances preferred Emery, gentle, rational, accepting. Mutual. Slyly she coughed for his attention and signaled for them to go home. He hesitated but then set his face to stay. All right all right go fly a kite.

A waiter moved among them like a matador, a towel over his arm, a tray of drinks poised for the kill. He was Filipino, colors of golden hills and black patent leather. The host called him Robert. Soon, Frances called him Bob. An hour passed and she called him Bobby. He said, Yes Mrs. Benedict, and she thrilled at the sound from strange luscious lips. Later, having crossed the hearth to the other window seat, she caught his eye. One enchanted evening. His white teeth gleamed for her. She played with the thought of lust. She saw them naked and exhausted upon hot sand but found that she had nothing further to say to him. To fill the void, she curried, combed, painted, filed, smoothed, roughed in order that she would want to talk to him. Why? Reality, as usual, impinged and she saw him sliding down the corridors of forever, happily passing drinks to friends of the rich. Let him climb some other snow-capped mountain. Poor Frances, she thought.

Two in the morning came none too soon and Emery, she thought, was none too sober. He did not so much approach as accost her. He took her elbow. She heard his trumpets blaring and the martial beat of his drums. He had not forgotten her, but he preferred himself. She was not defenseless but she was demanding. She reclaimed her elbow. At the front door he swooped down on a half-finished and deserted drink and after proffering it to her downed it with a flourish. His gesture was at once a reprimand, a warning, and a defiance. He apparently felt deeply guilty at having deserted her, but nonetheless he proclaimed that he was his own man by right, be quiet.

By reason and a long-standing agreement, she should have driven home. By happenstance she did not, for their host marched them down the stairs to the car. Before such a client as that, dear Emery lacked the courage to let her drive. She might have insisted, made a small scene, but she did not, out of pity and fortitude and a desire to justify all her grievances.

Gesturing grandly, drunkenly, Emery slid behind the wheel of the car and unerringly slipped the key in the ignition. Smiling grimly, Frances announced to herself that she was going to die on the Bloody Bayshore because their host wished, under cover of darkness, to pat her bottom one more time. She contemplated giving the old fool a punch in his belly and her resentment reached a climax. Is this the age we live in? No one counted her, protected her, nor was she free and equal. She wished ill on everyone.

As Emery bucked away from the curb, she looked back and saw their host sprawled face down in the entrance to his house. Now that, she said, will do for a starter.

"There's a stop sign," she said.

"I'm not blind," said Emery.

"Oh?" said Frances. She withdrew into her most maddening silence.

"Great party," said Emery, making amends. He glanced at her quickly as if to judge her mood. What right had he to smile who had no right not to smile? What gift was this? He drove, did he not?

"Absolutely tiptop, one in a million," she said. "Shall I drive?" She extended her hand as if literally to take the wheel.

He heard, saw, ignored. "They're first-rate people, really first-rate. Know what I mean?" It was his way of making friends, but he had no grievance.

"Well now let me see," she said. "You mean salt of the earth, don't you? May I drive now?"

Emery appeared to ruminate. "It's going to be a very fruitful relationship."

"He said you were the greatest lawyer since . . . John Jay. I'd like to drive, Emery."

He laughed. "That guy never heard of John Jay. I'm doing all right, ain't I? Driving?" His voice was so reasonable, not thick, just very careful and reasonable. He bore no grudge. He was, in fact, managing the car well enough. He had smoothed out the clutch and he traveled at moderate speed. All the same, she wanted to drive.

"In the early years of their marriage," she intoned as if reading from a document, "they agreed together, both parties complying without dissenting voice, that so-called role-playing was less important than life-living, that error would be on the side of over-safety, that should one or the other imbibe too deeply, that one automatically relinquished his or her rights to the wheel of the car, the body of the baby, the tray of Orrefors, or the handle of the hot pan. It was a bargain struck in good faith and high reason. It has no doubt saved them many a goblet."

"Agreed," he said, turning up the ramp to the Bayshore. "So?"

She had been acutely alert to him for years and she saw the components of his resistance, the pride, the threat, the daring, the fear. Nevertheless, it infuriated her.

"Tomorrow morning you'll give me that cute little crooked little smile of yours and you'll say Boy was I crocked last night, I didn't know whether I could drive home or not. If we live until tomorrow."

"Goddammit," said Emery, speeding up, "you know I'm not drunk but you just keep pounding away as if your life depended on it, just so you can win the round, just so you can show me."

"Merging traffic," she said.

"I see the merging traffic." His face became, for him, brutal and flushed. Suddenly he braked and swerved to avoid a sideswiping Thunderbird. His face quieted. "Got your seat belt fastened?" he asked in rueful apology.

She quoted a headline. "Lawyer and Wife Killed on Bayshore."

He thought he had her, he looked delicious. "*Prominent* Lawyer and *Beautiful* Wife Only Injured." When he heard himself, his smile soured. "Not injured either, dammit. Why do you act this way? What do you want?"

"I'd be mad as hell if I got killed coming home from a party as nasty as that one," she said.

At first he laughed at the absurdity of what she had said. And then he surrendered to her anger and its demands for combat. He drew back his lips and said, "You just can't stand it, can you? How many years and you just can't stand it when people are more interested in me than they are in you. You just got to cut me down some way."

Her skin felt like plaster of Paris and her teeth ached, but her voice was gay. "It's a man's world, you know. Poor Emery. Poor dear old Emery, with his hag of a nag of a bag of a wife. I mean, what the hell, if you want to drive while intoxicated, what difference does it make that I'll get killed too?"

Sour and silent, he drove the car. Stubbornly they built up the battlements of silence. The Bayshore swept down the countryside to the flat country and the bay and darkness. The hills to the right held pockets of light. A jet swooped upward from the runway at the airport. The moon vanished. Occasionally cars sped toward them on the other side of the parkway. Rarely, a car passed them heading south. Their own car began to lug. Emery gripped the wheel. He shifted down a gear. The car began to thud and bump. He switched off the ignition. Understanding struck them both but Frances rushed to speak it.

"It's a flat."

"I know it's a flat," he said, turning off to the shoulder of the road. "I am not a fool."

He applied the brakes and the car stopped. His face was sober and ashamed. She relented at the sight and wished to touch his face, give comfort, offer love and forgiveness. She devised a smile but not soon enough.

"You are so superior," he said. "You never had a flat in your whole life. You'd have seen the nail, whatever it was."

Rebuffed, she said warningly, "Perhaps."

"From you, that's a concession."

She knew that all he wished was one kind word, to be asked to share in the comedy or rue that lay beneath their quarrels. He was a bookish man, not a fighter. He hated to quarrel, as he inevitably, too late, proclaimed. She saw clearly, not for the first time, how she drove him to it, with her vanities and irritations, her untapped powers and her vast need for consolation. She saw, too, that he had not this time consoled her but had instead himself concocted a grievance. She refused then in all conscience to help him. Was it ever different?

"You may recall," she said, "that I asked to drive. Perhaps, just perhaps but nevertheless perhaps, we might have avoided this flat."

"Oh for Christ's sake stop it."

"But you had to show everyone how big and tough . . ."

"Can you stop it? Can you please stop it?"

"If I wanted to," she said.

"Can you forego just this one time the intense pleasure you get from hammering on me?"

"He said, hammering on her."

Her stomach cramped and her jaws ached, but she smiled to prepare herself for further battle. He was what he was, but so was she. She did not know what laws governed them. But loving each other (for all they knew or cared), they rubbed mild abrasions into deep rawness. Moments of contempt and anger had always come and gone, had often wracked and strained them to breaking, and always been inconclusively put away and forgotten. She was no fool, she of course wished for peace. But she said, "Can you change a tire?"

"That's helpful, that's real helpful," he said. "Leave it to you to make a man feel manly and confident."

He got out of the car, took off his coat and folded it neatly, placed it on the seat, rolled up his sleeves, loosened his necktie, and idly walked up and down beside the flat tire. Finally he got his keychain and opened the trunk. Staring ahead at oncoming lights, Frances listened to his work. She thought that she wished him success, but she was not sure. He removed the jack from the trunk and placed it under the back axle. Frances felt the car rise. She thought of going to stand with him but gave it up. They would only antagonize each other. She would create his mistakes. Once he had accomplished his task, he would be so happy that they would be friends again. He would be irresistible. If he succeeded.

She heard him bump the spare out of the trunk. He popped the hubcap off the flat tire. She heard his startled cry of pain. She opened the door and peered back at him. He held the heel of his thumb to his mouth. Blood darkened his arm and shirt front.

"Damn thing slipped," he said.

She took the handkerchief from his hip pocket and wrapped it around the wound. A car coming in their direction slowed. She raised her hand in greeting but lowered it in fear. Who were they and why? Emery turned, still holding his hand to his mouth. He looked at Frances, gleaming and relieved, as the car stopped behind them. Frances thought that she might herself have changed the tire. She feared strangers at such an hour.

Three young men got out of the car. They wore sports coats and white shirts and loosened neckties. They smelled of men's cologne and stale whiskey. They stopped before Emery and bowed low. Their manners were comic, impersonal, and threatening.

"Sir," said the shortest of the three, a boy of twenty or so with a crew cut and glasses. The largest one came to stand before Frances. "Madame," he said with a low bow.

The third boy said, "You talk entirely too much, bear," and all three commenced to laugh. Frances backed away. The big one did look like a bear, with his short arms and heavy torso and triangular head. A bear.

"I'm awfully glad to see you boys," said Emery. "I seem to have hurt myself." He presented his wounded hand for their inspection. The shortest one grasped it and shook it vigorously. Emery cried in pain.

"Leave off, Larry," said the third boy, apparently the leader. He was sharp-featured, yet soft and sensual. The other two, the bear and the one called Larry, watched and waited for his reactions. The three were, it seemed to Frances, a closed group, performers and audience at once. She and Emery were only props for them. Or toys. "Okay, doc," said the leader.

The bear approached Emery and extended his hand. He said, "I make no pretense at being adept at the healing arts but may I look at your wound?"

Emery held out his hand and the boy took it. He held the wound close to his eyes, pulled the handkerchief away and carefully pressed open the still bleeding gash in the heel of Emery's hand. Emery jerked away.

"What the hell, are you crazy?" he said.

"I wanted to see what was inside," the bear said.

"He's a sadist," said the leader.

"I was a teen-age sadist," said the bear. All three boys whooped with laughter.

"You boys run along," said Emery. "Find your fun someplace else."

Frances wondered where the highway patrol was. The vaunted highway patrol. Cars were fewer and fewer now.

The smallest of the boys, Larry, pushed his glasses up higher on his nose and after a glance at the leader walked to peer under the car. He put his hand on the bumper and gently, slowly began to rock the car.

"Stop that!" said Emery. With his hand at his mouth, he started toward Larry. The bear touched Emery's arm.

"He isn't hurting you, is he, mister?" The bear shot a glance at the leader. "Ever heard the story of the Good Samaritans? I mean, anybody else stop to help you? He's just trying to help, mister, in his own little way. Don't kill the instinct for brotherhood, mister, not in our Larry."

Emery paused. "He's going to rock the car off the jack."

"Larry ain't mean, mister," said the bear. "Ain't a mean bone in that kid's body."

"By accident, maybe," said Emery. He didn't look at anyone, nor did he move. Frances knew that he was uncertain and nervous, that he was unsure of how to handle the boys. He wouldn't want to act on impulse or do anything dangerous. And he did want the boys' help. He hesitated, staring at the roadway and sucking the wound on his hand.

"Larry ain't accidental, either, mister," said the bear. "Ain't an accidental bone in that kid's body. Is there, Larry?"

Larry turned toward Emery. He was not smiling, but his expression was trancelike. He began to shake his head, slowly, rhythmically, as if dancing. On that signal the other two boys also began to shake their heads, to wear trancelike expressions, and to move toward Emery. They moved in quite close, shaking their heads, but silent. Emery looked at the highway, up and down the highway. Frances said to herself that the boys were obviously kidding, that they would fold if Emery just showed a little authority, confidence. They were just kids. Clean kids, at that. Out on a lark. Showing off for each other. Not dangerous, not if someone laughed at them and said Fix the flat or go away. Emery said nothing. He did not feel comfortable or strong, perhaps it was his aching thumb, or the quarrel. Seconds ticked off. A car whipped past them.

"You want this tire fixed or not?" asked the bear.

"I seem to have hurt this hand rather badly," said Emery. He appealed to them with a smile.

"We ain't asking for a health report," said Larry. "You're taking too much time talking. You want the tire fixed or not?"

Frances said, "Yes," and Emery said, "Yes, if you would be so kind." His voice sounded choked and she knew he was angry to ask directly for help, from them. He had taken too much from them. She shrugged off the accusing look he gave her. If she hadn't said Yes, would he have said No? She didn't think so.

"We'd be delighted to be so kind," said Larry.

The bear walked to Emery and laughed when Emery backed off. "I won't hurt you, mister, not a mean bone in by body either. I don't want your wife to hear this." Emery looked suspicious but allowed himself to be involved. The bear cupped his hand around Emery's ear as if to whisper and he brought his mouth close. In a loud shouting voice he said, "You scared shitless, ain't you, mister?"

Emery jerked loose and Frances thought he was going to hit the boy. He stopped himself but his face clenched. "Now look here," he said, "you boys are having fun, but I don't find it at all funny. What are you up to, what do you want?" He looked from one to the other, demanding an answer, a rational explanation.

"Easy easy easy," said the leader in a soft sibilant voice. He held his hands up and shook them, as if to forestall Emery. He seemed deeply embarrassed. Emery went on.

"I say, if you are going to help, then help. If you are going to change the tire, then change it. But if you are going to rob, then rob. If you are going to hurt, then hurt. If you are going to . . ."

The bear interrupted. "Rape?" he asked.

"Shut up," said the leader. He gestured for Emery to go on, that he for one found Emery's words interesting and he was intent on listening.

"I'm sick of it," said Emery. "I've had as much of your clowning as I am going to. Either . . ."

"Inside," said the leader, gesturing toward the car door.

Emery did not answer. He stared as if he did not believe his ears. Larry took a step toward him. Spacing his words as if for a particularly stupid and stubborn person, he said, "Get in side. We will fix the flat. Get it?" He turned to the other two boys and then looked back at Emery. Very quickly he said, "The lady stays outside."

"Oh no," said Emery. He went to Frances and put his arm protectively about her shoulders. "Oh no," he repeated with finality. Larry went to the back of the car and began to rock it on the jack, back and forth, back and forth, with increasing tempo. He smiled sweetly, as if deeply engaged in the music of the rocking car. The bear began to move his hips and snap his fingers.

Emery pulled Frances farther away and then he turned back in fury to the boys. Frances put a restraining hand on his arm. His hands were locked in fists at his sides. She tightened her grip. She had thought the boys meant no great harm; but if Emery challenged them, would they be able to resist? What chance had a paunchy forty against three young bulls who were twenty and raging? Emery tugged at his arm but she held fast. Let them have their fun.

"Don't be a fool," she said. She pressed her body against his and forced him to move backward. They walked away from the car. She held his elbow and applied a gentling rhythmic pressure. She said, "They're just showing off. If you try to take them on, well . . ." She slipped her hand into his and they walked off hand in hand. Emery seemed blind and agonized.

"Christ!" he said. He stopped, forcing her to stop too.

She said, "They could easily rock the car off the jack. What could you do? You can't win. They could rock the car off the jack."

"Let them," said Emery. "I don't have to take their insolence."

She put her arms around him and leaned her head against his chest. He strained his head over her shoulder, asserting himself at the boys. Silently the boys watched and waited for Emery's next move, to play out their game against him and to defeat him. They despised him and Emery knew it and Frances knew it. But she thought it was useless for him to try to remedy their opinion of him.

"I'm in it, too," she said. "You can't just decide by yourself to start a fight."

"Start a fight Christ!" said Emery. He put his hands on her shoulders to shove her aside, but she locked her arms around his back.

"Get in the car," she said. "Please. For my sake. You aren't a child, proving something. What would be gained?"

"I don't know, something, I don't know." His breath was staccato, like obstructed sobs. Abruptly the strain left him and he grew slack, surrendered. She knew he was ready, needing now only a bit more persuasion. She wondered briefly, had it all been a charade, his willingness to fight? She did not dwell on the thought nor did she commit herself to it, but it was there. Automatically she marshaled the opposing force: his tension, his anger, his self-respect, and, of course, her own unfortunate instinct to comprehend the seamiest motive of everyone.

She said, "For my sake. Think what might happen to me. Those stupid toughs. Bully-boys. Bulls. Animals. Do it for my sake. Get in the car."

She urged him toward the door, her arms still locked behind him, as if they were dancing. He stared over her shoulder at the silent boys, from time to time made as if to challenge them. At the door of the car, she released her hold on him. Hesitancy gripped him and then he folded into the back seat.

The bear and Larry began to change the tire. Frances leaned against the front fender and drew her light jacket tighter. She felt quite chilled, and as she looked at the sky it seemed to recede and she seemed to shrink. She was on a vast empty darkened desert. She was delicate and exposed in a senseless universe and she was mortal and alone. All else was diversion, and useless.

She became aware of a presence near her and she was at once her intact self again. The third boy, the leader, had come to stand beside her, leaning, as she did, against the fender.

"You're a tough one, ain't you, a real tough one," he said. Polishing his teeth with his tongue, he nodded his head and looked at her under lowered lids. "I like tough women. Not cheap: tough. Know something? You ought to pick on somebody your own size, not a little guy like that one." He motioned with his head toward the car. "I bet not once, not once, you been with a guy as tough as you are."

How absurd, Frances cried to herself, how awful, she cried, and momentarily her body seemed to open wide and to close and she felt a chill on her neck and a tremble. As if by signal the boy pushed off from the car and came to stand face to face with her. He put his hands on his hips, thumbs hooked into his belt. He rocked back and forth, back and forth, from the balls of his feet to his heels, swinging closer and closer to Frances. He was grotesque, and lewd, a caricature, obscene, threatening, appealing. And she was herself and tough.

"You filthy little animal!" she said. "Don't dare touch me! You fix the tire and then leave us alone, all of you."

The boy laughed hollowly. "Tough," he said, "see what I mean?" He moved away and as he walked past the other boys he said, "Fix the tire like the lady said and then git." He shook a cigarette from a pack and went on to his own car. The other boys bent back to work. Frances felt the back end of the car go down and she heard the trunk slam. They were finished. With the leader at the wheel and without speaking or acknowledging Frances and Emery, the boys got in their car. Whatever they had wanted, they either had or would never have. Grinding, spitting stones, blowing smoke and the stench of burning rubber, the car sped away.

"They're gone," said Frances.

Emery's muffled voice came to her. "I hope you're satisfied. I hope one time in your life you're satisfied."

She did not answer. She knew what he meant, or thought she did, but she did not know what the truth was. After a moment she got behind the wheel and started the car. Slowly she gained the roadway and set out for home. Once home, she would consider Emery. She would help him. She would restore him with a final drink, with ice and coldness. She would persuade him, and herself, that really nothing important to either of them had been at stake. She would help him to discover the comedy of it all and to laugh. Slowly, between them, they would begin to build a little anecdote to relate to friends and to reduce the episode to dust. And in the darkness they would soothe each other's frail raw nakedness to a forgiving sleep. When they got home. But for now, as Emery wept silently in the back seat, she drove the car and she was exhilarated.

Night Guard

" 'Man's age-old melancholy, the coming of autumn,' " said Mr. Fisher, looking around the table at his daughter Charlotte and her two children. "That's Whitman, I think." He knew he had the thought, suitable for the evening, but had he quoted the words just right?

"The roast won't be worth eating if you don't go ahead and carve, Papa," said Charlotte, sitting at the other end of the table. She said it offhand, giving information, but it got to him. There she goes, he thought. What pleasure does she get from always telling me? She was a large full-fleshed woman going smiling, he remembered once telling her, through a pale-pink middle age and always talking on tiptoe. He knew that trick all right. Meant it was he who picked the quarrels every time. The way good women got their way. She was a good woman, but he was not to be bullied by her or anyone.

"Come to think of it, it's not Whitman, it's Bryant," he said.

His grandson Adam clattered his knife and spoon together, an impatient gesture hidden under cover of accident. Enough for Mr. Fisher to notice, but not enough to justify noticing. The family took so much of his time these days, just thinking about them, figuring out their whys and wherefores. They were so close he couldn't simply accept them as he once had, he had to understand them and guard against them. Guard against them, wasn't that a comment though? That was the trouble with retirement, too much intensive cultivation, you might say.

Yet it wasn't all bad. In spite of these irritations, he liked the company, and he liked most of what he knew about them. Especially Julia, he thought, turning to look at her. There she was, deciding between Whitman and Bryant, and knowing the difference too. Plenty smart for eighteen. Black-haired and blue-eyed, small and quick, just as he had been. She seemed more his own daughter than Charlotte's, and more than Charlotte was or ever had been. And when she teased him, as he knew she was fixing to do, turning her head so that what she said would sort of slide at him, it made him feel as alive as a young man.

"Whitman never was old enough to make a remark like that," she said. "It must have been Bryant." He made a swipe at her with his napkin and laughed and was about to reply in kind when Adam said, "I'm getting hunger pains, Grandpa. Are we going to eat or aren't we? Man ate before he ever read poetry, you know."

"Yes," said Mr. Fisher, feeling his old quickness working for him, "and he lived in trees and had lice and wore bearskins instead of those smart tweeds you've got on. So what does that prove? And besides," he went on, "I'm getting mighty tired of carving. Night after night. Why, I suppose I've carved 5000 roasts in my day." Before the words were well out, he regretted saying them, regretted his tiredness that brought them out. He could feel the family moving in on him, grabbing what he said as a sign of surrender.

"It is a bore," said Charlotte, cheerful and indifferent as if they hadn't been tussling over that one for months. "Let's have it done in the kitchen."

"A handsome piece of meat should be seen whole," he said.

"The man should carve," said Julia. "He should stand up and carve."

"I could do it," offered Adam.

"No," said Mr. Fisher in his hardest voice. "I'm the one to do the carving and I'm the one's going to." So that was that. He didn't mean to be rude but they pushed him so. It took all he could do sometimes to refrain from asking Who buys the meat? Who pays the bills? Who supports the household? Charlotte had forgotten her promise, made when she brought her two children home after she was widowed, that he was to take care of her and not the other way around. Let's get it said now once and for all, he had told her, it's my house and I'm in charge. We won't mention it again. And he hadn't, in spite of provocation.

He picked up the carving knife and tore at the roast so viciously, the knife whacking instead of slicing, that it divided, fell apart in no time, and he knew, without looking up, that Adam and Charlotte were searching out the small pieces of meat he had slung out on the white tablecloth.

"Adam," he said, passing him a plate, "you left the car unlocked again last night."

"Nobody's going to take the car."

"Take it or not, I want it locked."

"No sense making it too easy," said Julia.

Adam turned to her. "Then you lock it," he said.

Although Mr. Fisher knew the retort was really meant for him, he waited for Julia to answer.

"When I drive it, I do," she said. Airy voice showing the steel within. "It doesn't take much effort. You just turn the key. Grandpa wants it locked, lock it."

"That's right," said Mr. Fisher, lifting his hand to silence the deeper quarrel that might emerge. "It was long about 2:00 that I woke up. I never sleep through the night anymore." He knew he had said that before, but it had been true before and he refused to be ashamed. Then, remembering back, they were hardly with him, it was just himself alone and the dinner hour had turned to 2:00. "I heard something, like somebody tinkering around the car, and I went out to see. I didn't turn on the light, just slipped out to the front porch. I'm certain someone was there. I saw a shadow on the other side of the car." Then he was back at the table, bringing memory's residue of his fear and his pride. He felt himself beginning to smile. "So I just went out to the car and all around it. Whoever it was must have run off. I guess I scared them off. But the car door was unlocked, Adam."

"You went out to the car at 2:00 at night in your nightshirt?" asked Charlotte, looking grieved and scandalized.

"Don't fret, the neighbors didn't see me." He winked at Julia when she laughed at his joke. "Adam, I want you to . . ."

". . . lock the car door," finished Adam. His bland heavy face took on an unaccustomed worry. "All right, I will, Grandpa. But you shouldn't be out on the streets that late by yourself. Somebody might clout you over the head."

"You might catch cold," said Charlotte.

"Between you and the car, let them have the car," said Adam.

"Why, I thought you put a higher value on that car than that," said Mr. Fisher.

"All right then," said Adam, turning red. He began to eat with fury.

Mr. Fisher felt a little ashamed. "Take a joke, son," he said quietly. "You should know when a man's joking. I appreciate your concern. Though it's misguided."

"No," said Charlotte, "it is not misguided. Adam is quite right. You might get hurt out there."

"Hush," said the old man, "I had my gun." He opened a biscuit and breathed in the fragrant steam. He loved biscuits, nice soft pads to melt the butter on.

"What?" asked Charlotte.

"You what?" asked Adam.

Julia looked at him and shook her head in warning, as if to say Now just listen, you shouldn't have told them that. She was quick to know where the talk was headed, and quick to avoid unnecessary commotion. Like him in so many ways. But sometimes she didn't know when commotion was necessary.

"Did you decide between Bryant and Whitman?" she asked.

"Wait," said Charlotte. "You say you had your gun. What gun?"

"It was Bryant all right," he said. He turned to Charlotte. "I keep my .38 under my pillow nights, so I wasn't afraid. So no call for you to be." Yet, perhaps it would have been better not to tell them. Why did they challenge and push him so, to say things better left unsaid?

"Now really, Papa," said Charlotte, moving in fast. "That's extremely dangerous. It's unbelievable. A gun. Now really. I mean. Suppose you did see somebody, what could you do wouldn't make it worse? That's when you'd really be in trouble. That's when it'd really be dangerous. That's when . . . really."

"If I saw somebody," said Mr. Fisher, "I'd shoot is all I'd do."

"Shoot?" said Adam in a low shout. "You can't go around shooting every time you see a shadow or something. Good Lord. Suppose it was a neighbor? Suppose it was me? Good Lord." He thrashed a moment in his chair, looking exasperated, the old man thought, as only a bland, usually good-natured person can. His mother's son. Once aroused, a herd of cattle to stop.

"How many times have I shot you so far, Adam?" he asked. "Don't be a fool."

"But your nightmares," said Charlotte, keeping a level reasoning voice. "You're liable to wake up shooting. I didn't even know you had a gun. Much less . . . under your pillow. Carrying it out to the sidewalk. Now really, Papa."

"Come on now," said Julia. "Every man has a gun."

Her mother shot her a silencing look. "You know how you are, Papa. You have those terrible nightmares. I can hear you way at the other end of the house. And with Adam and Julia coming in so late. . . ."

"I am not going to shoot Adam and/or Julia. I am not a complete fool. Yet. So let's have no more of this nonsense," he said, letting the tone of final command come into his voice. That would stop them once and for all. "When I came to this town sixty-one years ago, every man-jack here carried a pistol in his hip pocket. And times weren't as bad as now. Not near as bad. Why, I bet not one of you read the evening paper about that murder not two miles from our doorstep. Armed robbery. Killed a filling station man didn't even have a gun."

But they wouldn't be distracted, their thoughts were stuck. They knew he wasn't to be bullied, it was senseless to try, but they registered their protest with silence. He turned to Julia and said, "What do you think? They do so much talking you haven't said a word and after all you're one of the ones going to be shot."

Julia put down her fork and she spoke so quickly he thought she had been planning it all along. " 'Always the loud angry crowd,' " she quoted, " 'very angry and very loud, Law is we.' " She turned to him and looked, he thought, as if she had swallowed a dozen canaries. " 'And always the soft idiot softly, Me.' "

"Don't be rude to your grandfather," said Charlotte.

"You call that poetry?" asked Mr. Fisher.

"I call it Auden," said Julia.

"And I call it words words words. They ought to put some of these young poets back in the oven a while. They need more baking."

"Young? Auden?" said Julia. "Come on, Grandpa, Browning wasn't the last poet in the world."

"Who said he was? Who said he was?" Mr. Fisher rushed to say. "I've never been afraid of the new and you know it. If it's good. Because I don't happen to like your Mr. Auden doesn't mean I'm an old fogey. But the trouble with you," he went on, wanting to sting back a little, "is, you're afraid of what's old and tried and that's a fact. If it's old you just automatically think it's no good, not worth your fooling with. It's got to be brand new for you else you just dismiss it."

"You're old," she said.

"What do you mean by that?" asked Mr. Fisher quietly.

"I don't notice anybody around here able to just dismiss you," she said, laughing, and he felt her laughter like the lifting of night. "You'd just go up and get that gun or something."

"That's right," he said. And he thought of what to say so quickly that he was amazed with himself. "That's my last granddaughter painted on the wall, looking as if she were alive." He was filled with a rare sense of rightness and he smiled at each of them.

He woke sitting straight up in bed, his fingers pressed against the bones of his face. The covers were a turmoil, half on the floor, half twisted around his chest and shoulders and chin. Then it came back to him. Someone was beating him about the face and head. He was a small boy and it was late night and someone was beating him about the face and attempting to smother him with the covers.

He looked around the room, not sure, even awake, that it had been only a nightmare. The thin arms of the clock, a pale misty green in the darkness, registered 11:37. He had been in bed hours, asleep at least two. Why the nightmare? What had awakened him?

He turned his head sideways off the pillow, heard nothing but the soothing murmur of the clock. He lay back and sighed, waiting to relax and calm down. His was a silent insulated room, down the hall, separated by an unused bedroom from where the others slept. And familiar to him, containing his things from years of accumulation, his huge dresser with the peeling mirror, his cracked marble-top table he could reach out and put his hand on, his double bed with its tall headboard of rough soft wood carved into knobs of roses and leaves. What a lot of excuses and subterfuges they found to get him to throw the thing away, the ugly thing. The ugly thing he had had for fifty years or so. He reached above his head and searched out the very center of the headboard, a monster splintering rose he could, and did, put his finger in up to the first knuckle. Himself again, he got out of bed to smooth the covers.

As he pulled the sheet up and took hold of the blanket, he heard the sound. He straightened at once, letting the covers slip from his hands. It came again, a rubbing sound like a shoe sliding over carpet. The house creaked, settled, the boards whimpered.

Someone was downstairs. The thing he had long dreaded and expected and listened for and waited for each night had happened. A stranger was in the house, would enter the rooms in silence and darkness, rob, rape, murder. And there was no one to stop him. No one except himself.

He forced himself to bend down, reach under the pillow and drag out the gun. It was cold in his hand and slippery from the moisture of his palm. But as he wiped the handle with the sheet and released the safety catch, the miracle happened. The surge of strength. The concentration of purpose. All right, he whispered, all right. He slipped his feet into his slippers, buttoned the top button of his nightshirt and opened the door with his left hand. His right hand held the gun.

The hall was almost in darkness, the night light below threw long dim shadows along the stairway. Quietly—there was only the sound of the back of his slippers slapping softly against his heel—he made his way down the stairs.

On the last step he paused and listened. A breathing sound, faint, as if deliberately through the mouth. He was sure it came from the dining room. There might be two, he thought, there might be more than two. I might not see in time, act quick enough. Then what? Now stop that. Stop that.

He forced himself to step off the last step, slide one foot in front of the other over the carpet. His step was uncertain, each foot, as he slid it, wavering, resistant, rebelling against his control. And his arms, hands, neck, tongue, lips turned resistant, moved each by a command of its own struggling against his command to go forward. And then he himself wished to turn back, to sneak up the steps to his bed and rejoin his sleep.

The gun. In time, before turning, he remembered that. He held the butt in one hand, the barrel in the other, and pressed the tip of his little finger in the barrel. What could they have more potent than the gun? What could they do he could not do first and better? What were they he was not more? Everything came together and he ceased to tremble. He drew his arm up until the gun was straight out in front of him, his finger firm on the trigger. Turning the knob of the dining-room door, throwing out his foot to kick it open—gun poised, finger ready—he shouted:

"All right, all right, I'll shoot."

It was Julia. The picture was distinct in the light of the dining-room chandelier he had not noticed (did no light seep over the door, none under, none around? had he simply failed to detect that obvious sign of innocence, failed to save himself this sudden agony by noticing?): Julia, the book propped against the squat candelabrum; the glass of milk; scattered sheets of paper. A picture he might, if he had only thought to, have imagined, almost seen through the heavy door. Julia's head came up at once, ducked down, her shoulder jerked up, warding off the expected blow. It hardly looked like Julia, always so gay and clean, now furtive and frightened.

"Grandpa," she cried, "it's just me."

"I know," he said.

He dropped the gun to his side and tried to conceal it in the folds of his nightshirt. He felt his face warming and his eyes clouding, and the sharp picture blurred. He felt, rather than saw, her startled eyes upon him, seeing the thin absurd sticks of his legs, his absurd fluttering nightshirt, his loose-skinned old face, the gun. He knew how she saw. He saw it so himself.

"I thought . . ." he began. What should he say?

Julia looked away, set aside the glass, closed the book, pushed the candelabrum from her, seemed deliberately to compose herself. She's just a child, he thought. She's still a child.

"You heard something," she said, calm, matter-of-fact, a voice he quickly hated. "But even so, Grandpa, you oughtn't grab that gun and come running. You might have shot me or something. You might have fallen and shot yourself."

"I did not," he said.

"Might," she corrected him. "Suppose I'd maybe just cut off the light or something. Suppose I'd been walking around in the dark. You might have shot me."

"I wouldn't hurt you, you know that."

"Not deliberately," she agreed. "But be reasonable." She smiled and he could feel it coming, the voice on tiptoe. "You've always been the most reasonable man in the world. The soul of reason. Now haven't you? With your nightmares and those bad eyes of yours. And that gun. Suppose it just went off. Accidentally."

The soul of reason. The putting of it like that made it seem not so. Don't talk to me like that, young lady. "I heard something," he said.

"This isn't like you, Grandpa. You've never been afraid before. You've never kept that gun so close. Why, even that summer we spent in the middle of nowhere you kept it in the trunk, not under your pillow. Remember? So now why?"

"Because . . ." he began, but he couldn't explain. Lamely, even knowing it would be the wrong thing to say, he said, "Somebody might hurt you or Adam."

"Let us take care of ourselves," she said. "Adam's six inches taller than you and forty pounds heavier. Let him take care of himself."

"He's just a boy."

"A boy? At twenty-two? You told me that when you were twenty-two . . ."

"Yes." He knew it was useless to go on. For her, for now, he was hopelessly in the wrong. His mind took another tack. Dangling him on my knee, giving him fifty cents for a movie, teaching him to drive the car, sending him to a fine school. For what? For this? And now her. "You think I'm foolish, too," he said. That ought to bring her up.

She said, "Promise me, no more cops and robbers."

Her hand under his elbow, she guided him through the doorway, and snapped off the light in the dining room. There was only the night light burning and the hall was quiet and hazy. Quickly he drew the gun up, closing Julia's hand in the crook of his elbow.

"Now what?" she asked. "What is it now?"

"Nothing." He dropped his arm to his side.

"It's all right. There's no one in the house. Just us."

Her fingers tapping reassurance on his forearm revived him and he jerked away. So she did think he was an incompetent, an old fool, ready for the trash can. He would not stand for that from her, from any of them, and he would tell her so. He felt anger beginning, but it was too strong, he knew, to be authority, too weak to be force. He had learned not to act in such a balance. Yet so often how he felt it. At a better time he would tell her that he would not stand it.

At the landing of the stairs he stopped and drew back the curtains and gazed out over the housetops, vague below him, to the lights of the city. Julia stood at his side, looking as they had so often looked out of that window, enjoying their small view, and it seemed to him that there would be no better moment to bring her back to him, to save her from the conspiracy. He thought for a ripe quotation.

"You say you know everything, Julia," he said, making his voice a teasing challenge. "Tell me where this is from: 'Now fades the glimmering landscape on the sight, And all the world a solemn stillness holds.' " He grinned at her, cocked his head, waited for her to invent a smart sassy answer.

"I don't know," she said. "Where?"

"Oh," said the old man, hurting with disappointment. "I guess you don't know everything after all, I guess you're not as smart as you claim."

"I guess not," she said. "Where's it from?"

But the name was gone and he was confusion again. He glanced out the window, saw that it was mostly only darkness and night and the trees were bare. He let the curtain drop.

"Where's what from?" he asked. Too late, he knew what. "Oh, it's from . . ." But the name wouldn't come. "I don't remember. I forget."

"Everyone forgets," she said.

"I'm an old man, my memory's pretty dim." With that, a turn he had never taken before, he felt himself grow weak, and he wanted her arm around him. And he hated her, as he hated Adam and Charlotte.

"Let's go on to bed," she said, taking his arm again. Easily, without his noticing for a moment more than a beginning sense of absence, she slipped the gun from his hand and held it away from him. Was it Julia? He would not have believed it, that she would even want to take his gun, never that she would dare. Had she changed so much, and he hadn't even noticed? Yet each plan he had to defend himself and regain the gun—points, quarrels, fights, commands flowed through his mind—turned foolish to him, weak, without dignity, unlike himself. Silent, still planning, he followed her the rest of the way up the stairs and into his room.

"Grandpa, sleep well," she said after she had smoothed the covers and he had obediently gotten into bed. Then, with decision, she said, "It just has to be this way." She leaned toward him, lips formed to kiss, but he shook her off, brought his shoulder up between them and caught the kiss on the tip of his ear.

"Now give it to me, Julia," he said, "and you go right on to bed. You've teased enough." He waited a moment and then went another way. "Every man has got to have a gun. You said so yourself. I don't want to get angry with you, but that's enough. Now."

"I'm sorry," was all she said, moving toward the door.

He realized his mistake. He had been too easy with her, coddled her, encouraged her to impudence. "Give me that gun," he said, barking each word. In total rushing anger he snapped his fingers and slapped his thigh. She had pushed him too far and now she would see. "When it's you gets scared that's different. Is that it? Are you a coward, scared over nothing? Scared at the sight of a gun? When Adam acts like a fool, you think it's funny. But when you act like a fool, you pretend it's because I am a fool, a senile old fool."

"Don't, Grandpa."

"At least Adam's honest about it. By God, give me that gun. If you don't put that gun on that table before I count three . . . Julia, Julia."

She turned off the light. "Good night," she whispered in a voice cracked and shrill with tears. She closed the door after her, and at the sound of the tongue of the door clicking into place and in the sudden darkness of the room, his anger fell apart. She was gone and with her she had taken his gun. Kindly. Even in his mounting fear he knew she meant to do kindness. Not mean or angry, she had simply walked out holding his gun. But without it how could he endure, face up, challenge?

He fell back against the pillows, drew his knees close to his chest, his body pressing deep into the mattress. Sudden sweat rolled down his temples and wet the edges of his check. He pulled the sides of the pillow up around his ears and pressed tight with his fingers. He heard the creak of the floor, the muffled closing of a door, the strange sounds of night.

Oh Jerusalem

Uncle Moishe-Moses-Morris-Maurice was sitting on the sofa with his feet flat on the floor and his hands lightly on his knees. He gave the impression of having waited for us in that pose for a long and trying time. Plump and nervous, he was like a bumblebee poised on a sofa.

Ours was a visit of duty, a time to be endured, undertaken solely out of a sense of behaving rightly. Uncle Maurice and Aunt Sarah had claims on us through my husband's dead father, Aunt Sarah's brother. I had never before met either of them, but of course I had heard about them.

Uncle Maurice was an embarrassment to the family and a comic figure to the world. He was full of words and postures, wit and foolishness. He was both volatile and calculated and no one trusted him. At the funeral of my husband's father, Uncle Maurice had planted himself in the very center of grief, mourned loudest and longest and lamented that he had lost even more than the dead man, his brother-in-law. But more than brother-in-law: his other self, his self-respect, his conscience. He used exactly those words and for some members of the family he made sorrow for a good man a false and shameful thing.

As for Aunt Sarah, best to say that she was a woman who had a great deal to put up with and did not always do it gracefully.

When William and I had married, four months before our visit, quietly and away from New York, we had received a telegram from

Uncle Maurice. "Your father would say, If I forget thee, Oh Jerusalem, let my right hand forget her cunning." William had assured me his father would have said no such thing. But I felt the telegram to be intentionally threatening and yet clownish.

Back in New York, we had made a series of calls on William's family, for me to see and be seen. They were pleasant undemanding little calls, perhaps to be repeated once a year. Uncle Maurice and Aunt Sarah had been slow to invite us and so when they finally did, for a Sunday afternoon, we were quick to accept.

"You see," said William, "they don't object so much."

What we had thought they objected to was the fact that William had married a Christian.

Once sure that we had seen his expectant waiting pose, Uncle Maurice rushed toward the front door of his apartment and held out a hand to each of us.

"Me," he said, "I'm glad to see you, I don't care what." As if according to plan, he shoved us urgently toward particular chairs on either side of the sofa, nodding and smiling all the while. "Sit down. Sit down. Let's not stand around all day, in my house there are plenty of chairs."

Aunt Sarah, taller than he and equally plump, had remained at the door, still holding the knob. Uncle Maurice had jerked us out of her care and she resented it but apparently had no recourse but to join the group, which, finally, shaking her head, she did.

"It's an honor to have you here," said Uncle Maurice. "It isn't every day our nephew the doctor visits us. He's a busy man." He looked at William shrewdly, assessing the damage of his thrust, and then smiled. "And yet when I see the son I think of the father, a man I loved better than a brother. I forgive the no visits."

"He was my brother," said Aunt Sarah.

"We were boys together," went on Uncle Maurice. "Born in the same town at the same time. He came to this country a year before I did. And three years later, my wife." He winked at Aunt Sarah and nodded. "But not then my wife, only his baby sister. She's been on my knee in more ways than one."

"I'm listening," I said, "but I can't hear any accent, at all."

He was pleased at that. "My youngest son says it's there. The accent. Still sometimes for fun I say born in New York and nobody calls me liar. Only a son could hear it. William's father came a year ahead, but you could hear the accent. Always the *w* was a *v*."

"Don't make fun," said Aunt Sarah. "The accent isn't everything." She sat quite still, with her fingers tensely and awkwardly at the belthooks of her elegant gray dress, and she watched her husband.

"Would I make fun of him?" asked Uncle Maurice. Shaking his head, pretending bewilderment, he turned to William. "Would I laugh at your father?"

"No," said William, in his thoughtful reassuring tone. "I can't think that you would. You were too close."

Uncle Maurice turned back to his wife. "Are we to have no refreshments, Sarah? You prepare all day for the visit and then we have nothing?"

"Nobody has prepared all day," said Aunt Sarah. "You talk too much."

Uncle Maurice laughed, happy with his anger turned to teasing. "You see, William? After twenty-eight years of marriage if I speak I talk too much. Unless I just say Yes ma'am. Train your wife early. A mean husband is a good marriage to these women. They don't like us when we're so easy."

"Easy," repeated Aunt Sarah. "My God. What would hard have been?"

William laughed, showing me the way to deal with this sudden ill humor. "Nothing changes," he said. "The same Uncle Maurice, the same Aunt Sarah, even the same old quarrel." We all laughed then, even Aunt Sarah. And indeed the quarrel seemed so old and so used and habitual that they were not ashamed and I was not embarrassed. Somehow the fact that they were relaxed enough to go on with their own relationship made our visit seem easier.

"That woman is Eddie Arcaro for twenty-eight years," said Uncle Maurice with pleasure, "and I am the horse. Your people wouldn't have stood it," he said to me in mock envy. "A bloody nose on Saturday night or Reno. And, God help us, some of us these days too. But

Alabama, not Reno. Down one morning and back the next, free as birds. We can't take time from our business, the almighty dollar, you think. Does marriage mean nothing these days? Bourbon or scotch? In spite of my wife I offer you my side of the refreshments."

"Scotch," I said, automatically. I looked at William, and with an almost imperceptible gesture of his hand he told me that he too had heard the almighty dollar but that we should both let it go by.

"Clever shiksa," said Uncle Maurice. "The scotch is at worst mediocre, but the bourbon, who knows? In this house you can be safe."

"All right, then," said William, "bourbon."

Uncle Maurice stood up and carefully worked his way around the coffee table and between the chairs. As he got alongside his wife, he invited us to watch his playfulness. He patted Aunt Sarah on the shoulder. "Pretending she has not been preparing all day the refreshments and then not bringing them out for us to enjoy. If we have refreshments, bring them out. If not, apologize and don't argue with your husband. Your own brother, our nephew's father, said how many times don't argue with your husband."

"He said a lot of things you don't follow either," said Aunt Sarah in a dull and graceless voice.

"Did he say don't feed your guests?"

With a face glinting with satisfaction, Uncle Maurice left the room. After a moment, Aunt Sarah followed him.

"The almighty dollar," I said, shaking my head.

"I won't let it bother me," said William, "if you won't let it bother you. We won't let it bother us if they won't let it bother them." But his expression was wary and I reached across the table to touch his hand.

"He's really not so bad," I said. "He's kind of cute."

"What a word," said William.

Uncle Maurice, bearing drinks, came back into the room. And shortly Aunt Sarah followed him. She was carrying a large silver tray, carrying it before her like an offering, not even allowing the edge of it to rest against her body. Little pieces of steak marinated for hours and broiled quickly in a hot oven. A plate of chicken sandwiches ice cold from the refrigerator. Cauliflower, carrots, celery and radishes, crisp and clean, carved and curled, and a lovely subtle cheese mixture molded into a double ring. The pride she felt in her skill and her strange shame of caring warred on her face. At first I was amused, then uncomfortable. Faintly William frowned. It seemed unfair that our casual visit, our visit intended only to manipulate their good graces, cost them so much. To make up for our indifference, we praised her highly, and regretted the condescension of that praise.

Uncle Maurice looked at the tray with pride. "That's my wife," he said. "A born cook but too proud to admit it. Eat up, eat up, and see what we are really like." Encouraging us with nods and gestures and example, he forced each dish on us and watched for our approval.

"Judge a man," he said, "by what he allows to go in his stomach. Me, I eat anything. I'm not prejudiced. Ancient laws I left in the old country. What I like, I eat. What I don't like, I don't eat and that isn't much. Jews are a fat people, you may have noticed, because we like to eat."

"I'm not fat," said William.

His voice fell on silence. Instinctively we both knew that his idle words were a mistake. Uncle Maurice looked at each of us, and at his wife.

"You have a shiksa cook," he said. "But for us none of your overcooked roast beef eaten only to get us to the next meal. We eat for pleasure and grow fat with pleasure."

"Why so proud right now?" asked Aunt Sarah. "You always tell me to reduce."

"I tease you," said Uncle Maurice sharply. "You can't take a joke. Every pound you have I'm proud of. Look at our niece, skinny as a rail. Not that I mind, I like it," he went on to me, "but your people think we're stingy and won't spend money. How account for our weight then? That costs money. I've had a thousand meals in gentile homes and gone away hungry. Eat, they said, but what was there to eat?"

"Please, Maurice," said Aunt Sarah. "Don't talk like that. He doesn't mean it."

Signals passed between William and me. Endure, endure, he said, it won't last long. I don't mind, I said, don't you. William gestured. A clown. Yes, a clown.

"Oh it was enough all right," said Uncle Maurice quickly. He leaned toward me, showing his good will. "The food, I'm not complaining, don't think that. They were my friends, the Christians, and I broke bread in their homes. Fine people, too, without prejudice, like yourself, like me. I was like a brother in the family. A step-brother. No, I don't mean that, I'm kidding, making a joke for my niece."

"It isn't a good joke," said Aunt Sarah. "Who can understand your jokes? Don't make them." She spoke in a warning tone and watched him with suspicion.

Uncle Maurice ignored her. "I don't say scratch a gentile deep enough and you find an anti-Semite. When we say that, we ask for it. It's our fault. I say scratch a gentile and if he itches you find a friend. It's a Christian world and if you find friends among them that's good. Walk careful and carry a big stick like the president said. But be willing. Not all Jews can do it. I can. They think they're too good for it. And when trouble comes they wonder why. They speak Yiddish in the goyim's faces and call them stupid. I say go to Israel or make friends, and who wants to hammer on sand? My nephew is a smart man, he knows the ways of the world. What's better than a friend? A little shiksa wife. Not that he married you for that, a girl like you. You're no fool. God grant we should have as clever among us. Not that we don't, don't get that idea, we do."

His words were coming too fast and I had no responses ready. William seemed as badgered and perplexed as I. We did nothing. We sat there listening and wanting not to hear.

"Maurice," said Aunt Sarah, in a tone that pretended to make light of what he had said. "Please, no more about mixed marriage. It's not a good topic. Accept it or don't accept, but let it alone. Too much talk talk talk," she finished, smiling sourly.

"I am not talk talk talk," said Uncle Maurice. "I am explaining. I want the shiksa niece to feel comfortable. If our nephew visited her family, wouldn't you want them to give him ease? If he visited."

"We visit," said William. "It's all right, don't worry."

"Well, then, maybe what my wife says is true," said Uncle Maurice, still rapid but now quiet. "Maybe the shiksa thinks I insult when I don't. For once maybe Sarah has a point. I'm a loudmouth, I guess. Look, I apologize, I've offended talking too much."

"No," I said, "Why should I be offended? Did I miss something? I like to hear you talk." William gave approval but Aunt Sarah, too late, shook her head at me, as if to say don't encourage him.

"See?" said Uncle Maurice. "A clever girl, like I said. Who knows what the goy thinks, but she says she likes to hear me talk and that's clever. And if she does, that's not only clever but wise. I'm just kidding. Look, don't you like chicken? Eat it. It isn't kosher."

"She doesn't mind if it's kosher," said Aunt Sarah. "She married a Jew, why should she mind? It isn't kosher."

"How do you know what she minds?" asked Uncle Maurice. "Are you an expert on Christians? And did she marry a Jew? Is this a Jew? He's no Jew, better to call him . . . look, I'm kidding. Making a joke at my nephew's expense." My husband is a placid man, he drank his drink in silence, not even requiring the satisfaction of a private smile. Uncle Maurice went on at once. "Your husband isn't my only kin married out of the tribe. The other was my own blood brother. Born in Poland same as me, but three when he came, a good age to come. It broke my mama's heart when he married."

"Don't talk about that now," said Aunt Sarah. "They don't care, don't start talking about it." She gestured aimlessly in the air.

Uncle Maurice flicked his fingers to silence her. "My mama said kaddish for him. Do you know what that is? Mourning, but it's the black of night. You think it was prejudice, but it wasn't. It was his age, twenty-one only and he would have made a fine rabbi. Who wants a rabbi with a Christian wife? With a doctor maybe it's different, maybe not. When the old people died we forgave him, our own flesh and blood, we wouldn't be prejudiced. He brings his family here once a month sometimes. Three beautiful children, blond as Norwegians. The wife is Norwegian. My God, my brother looks like a Norwegian these days, no one could accuse him of being a Jew. Smart kids, too, with the hands and with the head, a good combination. But are they Jews or Norwegians? My brother says who cares.

Not me. And now my nephew does the same. What is happening to us?"

William leaned toward him and put his hand on the arm of the sofa. "I don't know why you're talking like this," he said, "but it isn't pleasant for us. You know that. Aren't we welcome?"

Uncle Maurice looked alarmed and puzzled. With an effort he smiled. "I'm making a joke only," he said. "Kidding. Sometimes I don't make too good a joke. I like to be good-natured. And you're my favorite nephew. Not like a son but the son of a man better than a brother. Your father was not only my brother-in-law, he was a fine man in his own right. Talk about Christians, now he was a man they liked. Stop being a Jew, they used to say to him. Be one of us. But if I forget thee Oh Jerusalem, that was his motto. He's dead so I sent the wire myself, he would have said that. A hundred Christians walked behind him to his grave. And not debtors either. Friends. He'd give the shirt off his back, ten dollars if he had eleven. Nothing mean came from his lips. If only his sister was like that. But I made my bed and out of it came two fine sons. Both married now and none to shiksas, thank God. I beat him there."

I reached for a chunk of steak and ate it. It was a strange moment for me. I felt involved and yet irresponsible. I was sure that there was nothing I could do. Uncle Maurice leaned forward and cocked his head to look directly in my face.

"Now I've said too much and you're angry, little shiksa," he said. "You think I'm a bigot when I'm not. I don't care who my sons marry. Understand me. When Jews marry out, who is it to? Country girls and dyed blonds. For the money. I know. Not you, I know that. Don't take it personal. Why get angry? Be reasonable."

Aunt Sarah stood up. "Chicken sandwiches, everybody," she said. "Eat some chicken sandwiches." William and I reached for the sandwiches, our hands briefly touching. Abruptly Aunt Sarah sat back down, and when she spoke again, all pretense had left her voice, and it was hard and angry. "Be quiet, Maurice. You make it worse. Be quiet."

"That shows how much you know," said Uncle Maurice. "I'm not talking about our niece, I'm talking to her. If you had eyes you'd see we're friends already, the niece and me. She knows I kid her." He bobbed his head to encourage my answer. Chicken sandwiches saved me from speech and I merely smiled and nodded yes.

"You go out of your way to be insulting and ruin a pleasant visit," said Aunt Sarah. "I'm not suprised, I knew it. I said don't invite, it isn't necessary, but you insisted. All my life it's like that."

The quarrel was no longer easy and no longer amusing. I looked down at my lap and picked bread crumbs from my skirt and carefully placed them in an ashtray. Across from me William sat silently, his lips stiff, and I thought how much worse it was for him than for me. The undivorceable family, the burden of Uncle Maurice always on his back.

"You think it's all my fault," said Uncle Maurice. "Always to my wife it's my fault, and then she wonders I feel persecuted. Look. Listen to me. Where would my sons have found Christians? Who are they to know high-type Christians? My nephew the doctor, that's different. Merchants, what do they do, somebody comes in our little store looking for a bargain and six months credit? There's a line romance doesn't crawl over. Let's don't quarrel. I'm a fool, everybody knows it. Ask my wife, she'll tell you. Ask your husband, he remembers. Nobody pays any attention to me. I'm not a rabbi, I'm not even an elder, maybe I'm not a good Jew. If I offended, I'm sorry, I can't say more than sorry. I don't mean to talk like that, but there it is, out before I hear it in my brains. Your husband's father said to me, Maurice, if you would listen you wouldn't have such pain, you would see we accept you. So let your children be Norwegian. I don't care. I welcome them as my kin."

He paused a moment and as he paused I saw anger on his face and I felt once more that it was directed at me. "But do I hate my own people?" he asked. "If there's the choice to be scorned as a Jew or to scorn the Jew, I'll be scorned, by God. That doesn't scare me."

As quickly risen, his anger fell, and he turned to William. He seemed puzzled and beseeching. "There I go, I'm a loudmouth. Why can't I stop talking? Is it a disease?"

"I always tell you," said Aunt Sarah, her voice hammering across the coffee table, a menacing hard voice, "you should listen once in a while. Avoid pain with silence. Hear nothing. Say nothing."

"Who taught you that besides me?" asked Uncle Maurice, turning on her. "William's father was a silent man and married a talkative woman, a good balance. And I talk and who do I get? I get a talkative woman too, a bad balance. Is that fair? What is fair? He was loved by the Christians as a man, and by the Jews too. He never turned his back on his people or his religion. And my Christian friends, who are they? The bookie, the barber, the wholesaler. And the Jews, they think I'm no-good, a turncoat. Why should they care for me? I'm not like him, I'm a loudmouth. My nephew brings his wife here and I want to please her, to make a friend for myself. A pretty girl. A shiksa. But I offend her. I offend my wife. I offend my nephew. Jews and Christians, it doesn't matter. I'm a loudmouth. I'm nothing."

Aunt Sarah had been trying to interrupt him and finally she did. "I tell you now," she said, in a warning-charged overbearing voice, "be quiet now for good."

"Everybody be quiet," said William quietly, raising his hand in a slow silencing gesture. "This isn't good. You're hurting yourself. Please."

But neither one nor the other could be stopped. Aunt Sarah pulled herself forward on her chair and looked at her husband. Her emotions, like his, had their own irrevocable direction, and nothing William or I could do or say could stop the movement of her rage. We could only sit and endure.

"When we knew William and the girl were coming," she said, "I said don't talk about shiksas and Christians and goyim and mixed marriage. I'm no fool, I know how it goes with you after twenty-eight years. And you said you wouldn't. But you talk and talk, you can't not talk. You're a fool."

"A fool and a loudmouth," said Uncle Maurice with a startling shout of laughter. "A fool and a loudmouth, a Christian and a Jew all at once. That's a good one, a good joke. Which am I more of? Who knows? I saw the kind of world it was, a Christian world. Okay, a Christian in a Christian world, I said. That's what I said."

"Maurice, I say be quiet," said Aunt Sarah.

"Six churches on six Sundays," he said. "There I was, smelling of stuffed cabbage and sour cream. I was eighteen and they said you're welcome to be a Christian but they acted you're not welcome. So back I came, back to the Jews with my tail between my legs. You didn't know that, did you, William? You thought you were the only one wanted out."

"You're saying more than you mean," said William. "I don't want out. Let's change the subject. We're here only a short time. Tell us about your sons, tell us about them."

"No," said Aunt Sarah, "he can't change the subject. He doesn't care about anything. He has to talk until he makes a fool of himself and me."

"Is the truth foolish?" asked Uncle Maurice in a reasoning questioning tone. "Is it foolish to teach the young? I'm telling this boy from my own experience. Is it foolish to say no to a grilled ham and cheese and yes to stuffed cabbage? Why should I turn my back for a mess of pottage? The hands were the hands of Esau but the voice was the voice of Jacob. So back I came to the Jews, gladly. And when my brother, my blood brother, married a shiksa I said I know what it's like, don't go. But he went and he never looked back at us. He says a Jew is what a man believes, how can he say that? A Jew is a Jew. But he looks like a Norwegian these days. How could he go so easy? I couldn't go but my kid brother could. The truth is you can't be one of them so why try. They bolt the door and say don't come. And we say who wants to come. And who does? Besides my brother."

"Nobody," said Aunt Sarah. "Why accuse William? Why talk about it?"

Uncle Maurice turned abruptly to me with a gesture of both hands, half apology, half condescension, mixed as all his gestures were. "Not that I scorn the religion," he said. "A man believes as he believes and no matter so long as he believes. Me, I'm a free thinker. The business of hogs is hogwash, I say. That's a joke. I don't eat shellfish because I don't like shellfish. It's dirty. But miracles, raising the dead, that won't swallow. I tried and it choked in my throat. I like you, you listen. Can't they say fine man and let it go at that? But who knows beyond the grave. There are so many of them. And here is one in our own place, married to our nephew the doctor. Taking the best of us, the learned man. Sitting there thinking her husband's uncle is a fool and a loudmouth. Don't cringe, nephew, you pay your call from duty and you don't have to see us anymore. Forget the family of your father. Now you have cousins on the other side. Tillers of the soil maybe. Smart with the hands, but with the head? Remember what happened to Heine. On his deathbed back he came. It's in your blood. Centuries of the peddle cart. M.D. doesn't mean a thing. Now you peddle pills is all, a middleman to sell prescriptions to society ladies with little aches. You should come back to us with the big aches. I could tell you aches."

William reached over and shook Uncle Maurice's knee. "I'm not going anywhere," he said. "I haven't turned my back, I've only gotten married. Look, could I ever look like a Norwegian? Stop hurting yourself. Stop trying to hurt us. We've done nothing."

But nothing could be saved. Aunt Sarah rose to her feet and stood over Uncle Maurice in a posture of threat and wrath. "So our nephew only has Christians for patients? He refuses Jews? You set out to ruin the visit of my brother's son and you ruin it. Why? You can't be quiet?" She turned to me in another rush of fury. "My brother said don't marry him, I know him from the old country when you were a baby, he's a loudmouth with an itch to be what he isn't. But I was a fool, I wouldn't listen."

Uncle Maurice stood up, indignant and defensive. He stared at her for a moment, how silently he stared. "That is not so," he said in a voice of quiet and control. "He loved me better than a brother. You sour life for me, don't sour that. He accepted me for me. He alone accepted me. Let them all say I am a loudmouth and a fool, he loved me better than a brother. Quiet, Maurice, he said, easy, Maurice. He said, Be what you can, nothing more, nothing less, it's good enough. He didn't scorn me. When I was eighteen and came back ashamed, all laughed but him and scorned me. Oh, Moishe, you forgot Jerusalem, they said, they who remembered only the ghetto. But he whose heart was Jerusalem said, Be what you can, nothing more, nothing less. Be Moses if you can, but if not be

Maurice and don't blame yourself."

"Then why blame yourself?" asked William, so pained, so gentle. "He loved you better than a brother and accepted you. And we accept you. Don't blame yourself."

"So," said Uncle Maurice. He sat down again and looked at his necktie. "Your father, my brother-in-law, never turned his back once on his people. My own blood brother, he never looked over his shoulder after he walked away from the Jews. Was that hard? Be Maurice, is that easy? One son says I am not Jew enough. I should wear a skull cap and go to his fancy synagogue. The other son says I'm Jew too much, I should drop even Yom Kippur. So what do I do? What can I be? Just Maurice, neither more nor less. And what is that? Is that an honor?"

He sat quite still, only his crossed leg bobbing to the echoed rhythm of his voice. When finally in the silence he lifted his head, he looked sick and foolish and shrewd. And we were ashamed to see him.

As if she had been waiting for just that moment, Aunt Sarah went over to him. She put her hand on his shoulder, and I thought that that first kind touch was the goal, the inevitable purpose of all her rage, repeated endlessly over twenty-eight years of embarrassment and quarrel.

"Look, you'd better go," she said to us. "He talks too much and then he's ashamed and then he's tired."

"Is he sick?" asked William, their nephew the doctor. "Can I do something?" But he knew, as I did, that we were hardly in it.

"Is tired sick?" asked Uncle Maurice. He laughed and looked from William to me and he seemed to be mustering strength for another attack of words. "You paid your call from duty. Next time come to visit. No chicken sandwiches, we'll have gefilte fish. We're Jews, nothing more, nothing less, and proud of it. Accept us or not, we don't care. I'm not prejudiced. Who am I to judge my nephew and his wife. Judge yourself, but who can do that? We see people looking at us is how we judge ourselves. You think I'm looking at you but I'm not. I look only at the son of my friend and I smile at you as he smiled at me. You didn't choose easy, William, it isn't easy to be William, but remember Jerusalem. There I go, talking too much. But I'm not going to cut out my tongue if nobody likes me talking. Not my wife, not my nephew, not the shiksa."

"Be quiet," said Aunt Sarah, so quiet and gentle it hardly sounded like her. "Say goodbye to them, but don't talk."

Second Wind

Conrad's mother said, "Come to view the evening miracle?"

She sat at her dressing table in front of a large mirror surrounded by naked light bulbs. Conrad went to stand behind her. He wondered if staring through all that light would blind him the way looking at the sun would. His mother made a funny face at him in the mirror. He stuck his fingers in the corners of his mouth and pulled up his lips to show the gap where his new front teeth were beginning to come in. She laughed. After a moment, she looked at herself. She chose a lipstick from a row of tubes and put a pale color to her lips. She pressed her cheeks up and away from her nose and then rubbed her eyebrows with the tip of her little finger. She said to Conrad, "All right, Richard Burton, what's the verdict: am I beautiful enough?"

Conrad's father said, "Just to go across the road for the evening? Of course, I wouldn't know who'll be there." There was a stillness in the room. Conrad felt his breath quicken. He had forgotten it would happen.

His mother leaned forward to stare in the mirror and his father stared at the mirror and neither spoke. Conrad ducked down and he could see the lower part of his father's face, the reddish moustache and the colorful necktie and the shoulder of his dark jacket. He saw all three of them in the mirror.

"Thanks," his mother finally said. "Conrad, when you grow up, at least try to be tender and generous and loving."

"And thank you," said his father, "and try to have a loving wife."

When his parents went out the front door, Conrad went to the family room to be with the sitter, a neighbor girl of thirteen. She was angrily twisting the television knob from channel to channel. She whirled toward him. "I hate Saturdays, there's nothing, nothing, nothing."

In his dreams he threw a baseball high in the air out in the sunny pasture behind their house. He wobbled around under it, ready for the catch, his hand over his eyes against the high noon sun, but the ball fell into the living room and crashed against glass. He heard his father say, "The Steuben. That little gesture was worth seventy-five dollars." Before he could say he was sorry he heard his mother say, "But such a lovely sound, like ten thousand dimes falling on some of your priceless concrete. I'm glad I broke it." Their voices rose together and fell and rose again and he knew he was awake.

He sat up in bed and yelled, "Mother," and was immediately sorry. He should have listened for the sounds first and done his nose-breaths to be sure everything was all right.

They stood in the doorway with the light behind them. He could not see their faces. His mother said, "Hi, sweetboy, what's the matter?" Her voice was slurred. If he had only done his nose-breaths he would have known that and he could have put the pillow over his head.

His father said, "Just go on, I'll take care of him."

"He called me, I'm the one he calls mother, remember? Oh I know you'd like to be both. . . . Been awake long, sweetboy?"

"Yes, a long time," Conrad said. He thought they would be proud of that. He thought that perhaps he had not been asleep at all.

She came to sit on the edge of the bed and she pulled him toward her. "Poor baby, you should have called me when you first woke up."

His father said, "What good would it have done if he had, you weren't here."

Conrad noticed then that his mother had on her coat but his father was in pajamas. He said, "I need to go to the bathroom."

His mother picked him up and he put his legs around her waist and locked his hands behind her neck. She hitched him up a little and started with a lurch toward the bathroom. He was angry with her for drinking when she knew he didn't like it and he was afraid she would drop him, like the glass. "I can walk," he said.

"He's not a baby, let him walk," his father said. He put his hands under Conrad's arms. "You might drop him, you're drunk."

"Stoned," she said, "and maybe just a weeny bit high. A delicious mix, you should try it. It might do you some good."

"Let go, let me have him," his father said.

"Afraid I might break this little investment the way I did the Steuben?"

His father slapped her on the face. Conrad began to cry. "Please don't, please don't!" he said.

His father said, "I hope goddamn you're happy," and walked out of the room.

His mother said, "Well well well." Her face began to turn red.

After Conrad had gone to the toilet, she let him walk back to his bed and she lay down beside him. "Go to sleep, sweetboy," she said. She scratched his back and rubbed his shoulder. Just as he was dropping off, she said, "Wouldn't it be better if we stopped now instead of destroying each other."

Conrad said, "You don't have to destroy."

"Once you start . . . go to sleep now, it's not your battle. Just a civilian casualty. I wonder how I got to be thirty-five so soon and everything out there still untouched and I could touch it, I could do it all. Don't ever be afraid to be alive, Con. Take the chance, chase the wild goose, touch everything. Otherwise you dry up, you solidify, like concrete, like old man concrete himself. Then you might as well be dead. Massa's in the cold cold ground and he isn't even forty. Hello, Massa."

His father was standing in the doorway. "Don't you have the decency to let the boy sleep instead of poisoning him with your rot?"

She said, "I'm just telling him there's something besides after taxes and the school board election. Half the night on the tax structure and the other nine-tenths on the school, all those exciting teachers, those fascinating principals."

"While you were doing what that was more interesting?"

"Ah but wouldn't you love to know."

"You disgust me," he said. "Conrad, I'll say it to you: I'm very sorry I struck your mother."

"At least you're consistent," she said, "an old fogey all the way." He turned and walked away. She hugged Conrad to her. "My God what this must be doing to you. You know you're really all I care about. Obviously I mean in addition to me. But you. And not just to make sure you get into Harvard and Harvard Law and Harvard Business Machines. But are you happy right this minute. But am I? How much should a person give up for somebody else's being happy? Not that you would have to give up much. I must be high, talking this way. I don't want to turn you against him. He's a good father just as my father was a good father, although he couldn't recognize me on a downtown street in a crowd of three girls. But as my mother always said, a good provider. She used to sit up on that hill making friends with the servants and polishing her snuff box collection. She had a fantastic collection of snuff boxes. My God. Free at last, free at last."

Conrad saw her running across the pasture to the dark woods on the far side. "Are you going to leave me?"

"Never," she said. "Nobody's going anywhere. Don't bother your sweet head with stupid grownup stuff. Go to sleep." She turned him so that he faced away from her and then she fitted his body to hers and put her arms around him. He heard her sigh and he felt the breath of her sigh on his neck.

The sunshine woke him and he got dressed and went into the kitchen. Usually on Sunday mornings he got himself a bowl of cereal and a glass of milk while his parents slept. He turned on the television and watched NFL Highlights and a piece of a church service. When his parents came in at midmorning, he was watching some men talk about life in the city. He had been watching so long that he thought they would notice how swollen and watery his eyes were. But no one said anything except Good morning.

He looked from one to the other trying to figure out how they felt this morning and whether or not last night was still going on. Sometimes they were angry for days and sometimes their anger just stopped. His father had on blue jeans and a gray sweatshirt and sneakers and his mother had on old slacks and her hair was tied up behind and he knew they would stay home all day. Some Sundays the three of them went to visit friends and then everything was funny and they all had a good time and didn't quarrel. He thought that this wouldn't be a good day.

His mother said, "You seem awfully somber this morning."

Her tone seemed to blame him for it and he began to make an excuse. "I was watching this program a long time and it wasn't fun, it was really awful."

"I don't suppose it would have occurred to you to turn it off. Why do you waste your time with that stupid stuff?"

"I'm sorry, I won't any more ever, I promise." He meant it too; the only thing he really liked was the football.

Abruptly, she went to him and locked his head in the crook of her elbow. "Poor little sparrow. Do you know how much I love you?" She began to scratch his back.

His father said, "Even if nobody else does."

She stopped scratching before she caught up with the itch that ran across his back just in front of her nails. She said, "I thought we said we weren't going to."

"I guess that's right," his father said. He stared at the table. "I'm sorry."

Conrad went over to him. "Want to throw the football?"

His father said, "Maybe later. Why don't you go outside while the sun's shining."

The autumn sun barely took the cold off the midday air, but Conrad was glad to be outside. He would stay on his guard. If he listened intently he would be able to hear if there were bad sounds in the house, like the sound of the telephone wires when the wind blew, and if he took his nose-breaths, he would be able to smell the smell of whiskey and sour milk. And he would know.

He walked to the pasture to play One Flew Up with the children from down the road. He was cold and when he rushed to kick the ball he slipped and fell hard on his bottom. The children laughed and he was afraid he might cry and run into the house. He quickly put his hands on his bottom and did a little dance, rolling his eyes and shaking his hips so that his bottom jiggled. He thought he was a very good clown and that his mother would have been proud.

When the other children went into their houses for lunch, he stayed out and ran races with himself. He felt lonesome and hungry and so he went into his kitchen and broke a hunk of yellow cheese from the block and ate it with some crackers and root beer. He went into the family room and turned on the television and for an hour or so watched the Cleveland Browns defeat Cincinnati. When the game was over, he remembered that he had said he wouldn't watch television any more and he turned the machine off. He opened the door to the living room to see where his parents were and he heard his mother say, "If you're so damn sure, then you tell me what happened."

His father said, "If I were one hundred percent instead of just ninety-nine. . . ." Conrad closed the door. His mother called, "Is that you, Conrad?" and he went into the living room.

His parents sat on either side of the fireplace. Some Sundays they lighted a fire and they always had one when they had company. He picked up the poker and punched the cold ashes. The draperies were open, but the sunshine seemed to gray the blues and greens of the room and he felt cold. He said, "I wish we had a fire."

"We don't need a fire," his father said.

"It's cold out," Conrad said.

"It's cold in," his mother said.

"Want to throw the football now?" Conrad asked.

His father said, "Not now, maybe later."

"Maybe never," said his mother.

His father glared at him as if he had been the one to say it. Conrad said, "It's okay, you don't have to."

"No, I'll throw you a couple," his father said.

Conrad missed the first two throws because they were too high and hard but he caught the next four in a row. His hands stung but he was pleased with himself.

His father said, "You're really good. Let's go for the big one. Out twenty, count 'em off, then five straight right."

Conrad centered the ball and then loped out. He counted twenty and turned and the ball smashed against his cheek. His father said, "Sorry, but you got to stay alert."

Conrad said, "You told me out twenty and then five to the right." His cheek hurt and he was sure it would be swollen.

"I said I was sorry."

Conrad screamed, "Last night when you hit her you said you were sorry; you're always sorry." When he realized he was crying he tried to stop. He didn't want to be a baby. It hadn't hurt that much. His father ran to him and grabbed him in a big hug. "Don't cry, don't cry, everything's going to be all right, really it'll be all right." He took out his handkerchief and wiped Conrad's nose and eyes.

Conrad said, "Don't get my nose in my eyes."

They both laughed a little and then his father led him to the stump of an immense old tree that had been cut down. They sat side by side with Conrad in the circle of his father's arm.

"Look, son," his father said, "suppose you didn't have a father. I mean, suppose you only saw me weekends or something."

Conrad didn't answer for a moment. He wanted to please his father but he wasn't sure just what to say. Finally he said, "That'd be fine."

His father blew air through his nose in a kind of laugh and Conrad knew he hadn't said the right thing. He felt angry because he had tried to help and no one had told him how. He said, "Anyway, that's a dumb question. You aren't going to leave just because you socked her, are you?"

"No, no," his father said. "It was just a dumb question, like you said. Okay, come on, out twenty and then a little hook and stop. I promise this time."

Conrad said, "You don't have to throw any more."

"I want to, but let's try a little razzmatazz. Out twenty-five, then six to the right and then straight back oh say about ten."

"I can catch long ones," Conrad said. "I'd practically be back where I started."

"So it'll be a handoff," said his father. He still hadn't gotten up. "Vary the defense, keep 'em off balance, take a leaf from your mother's book of nonrules. You know," he said, tossing the football from one hand to the other, "I'm what I guess they call conventional. I'm not very loose or creative. I'm not witty or profound. I guess I'm not the world's most exciting guy. But I never was, I'm still the same me, I haven't gotten any worse."

He tried to twirl the football on his index finger but it kept dropping off. Conrad knew his father wanted something from him but he didn't know what it was. His mother always seemed to tell him what she wanted, but his father just sat there, wanting.

Conrad said, "I think you're exciting. Anyway, I don't like excitement."

"I have a lot to offer, goddammit," his father said. "At least you can count on me, I don't shirk. And don't tell me things don't matter any more. Not if you have them they don't. This house, two cars, the place at the lake. She acts as if it's some kind of sin to make a useful in fact essential product and get some kind of recognition for it. I don't think people ought to talk to their kid about the other one even if she does. But I'm just having a talk with my son about me. My father never talked to me. Died at sixty-three but he always seemed sixty-three to me. She thinks she invented not wanting to get old and stuck but you have to grow up sometime." He stopped speaking and sat on the stump balancing the football.

After a little while, Conrad said, "Will you throw me the long one now?"

"Sure, the big bomb. Out thirty." His father put his hands on his knees as if to get up but then he grabbed Conrad and said, "Do you like me?"

"Yes," Conrad said, "I like you a lot, I really like you."

"Thank you." His father stood up. "Now for that bomb." He held the football on his forearms and pretended to spit on his fingers and then he rubbed his hands together. "A real bomb, a tie-breaker, a game-winner."

Conrad centered the ball and ran straight out thirty giant steps. His father drew back his arm and threw. The football was wobbly and a little short and off to the left. It was all Conrad could do to even touch it. He hated to end on a failure. He thought his father owed him another chance. But when he had retrieved the ball and turned, he saw that his father was moving toward the house.

The sun was below the tops of the pines and on the road in front of their house cars zoomed by with their headlights already on. Conrad threw himself high flies with the football and when he caught one he zigzagged across the broken field for a touchdown. No one could catch him. He was a fine runner and he decided to go to the schoolyard to show off his great running.

He cut across the pasture and down the road just as he did every day. He thought he ought to tell his parents but he decided not to bother them. When he got to the schoolyard, no one was there. He played on the bars for awhile but the coldness of the hard metal hurt his hands. He walked around the school and tried a few windows to see if he could get in. The windows were all locked. He climbed the fence that ran along the building and he tried to reach the overhang of the roof so that he could climb up. He reached too far and lost his balance. He landed on all fours and he thought, Suppose I had been too hurt to move.

It was dark, the real dark, and he didn't have an excuse for being out. He imagined that he was badly hurt and could not walk on his broken ankle. His parents came looking for him and brought all their friends and the neighbors and the police, and all the children in the school. His parents both hugged him and they both kissed him and they took him home to his warm bed in his bright room and he ate milktoast and soft boiled eggs just as he did when he was sick. His parents stood at the end of the bed and smiled at him over the footboard. They were so grateful to have him and their faces were clean and bright and they were happy.

He stood up and listened intently but he didn't hear the bad sounds at his house and he took his nose-breaths and he smelled only the cold. He began to run home. When he crossed the pasture he realized he had forgotten his football but he decided to leave it there until morning. As he ran he wiped his nose on the sleeve of his jacket and rubbed his eyes with the knitted cuff. He ran toward the lights.

When he got inside he took off his jacket and rolled it inside out so his parents wouldn't see the streaks of runny nose. He went into the bathroom and washed his face and hands. He wanted everything to be just right.

They were sitting in the same chairs in the living room but someone had made a fire. The flames leaped between them. That was a good sign and their faces did not seem so stiff and staring, and that was a good sign too.

"Come in, sweetboy," his mother said.

"I made your fire," his father said. "Sit down, there's something we want to tell you."

Conrad went to stand in front of the fire and the fire so quickly warmed his skin that he began to feel the deep deep cold inside and he thought that his bones were made of a hard cold metal. He said, "I know."

Once a Thief . . .

Virginia Connelly heard the snap of the shade against the window frame and the swish of organdy curtains and she rejected the sounds as each morning she rejected the first sounds. This time she was fairly sure she was right. She had arrived at her sister's house late the night before and she had gone straight to bed, straight to sleep, straight to hell and now back.

What she next heard she could not reject, a squeaky voice saying, "It's me, Aunt Virginia."

"Don't call me aunt. Just call me plain Virginia. I mean, Virginia. You don't have to call me plain either."

The next voice, open, firm, modulated, a voice she had often called The Honest Voice: "Don't bother Aunt Virginia, Kate."

"Don't bother Virginia," said Virginia. She opened her eyes with elaborate slowness and saw the two of them standing at the foot of the bed, framed like valentines by the tester. Her sister, smiling, handsome, clean, barefaced. Her niece, owl-eyed and curious, shamelessly watching. "It's all right to bother me, but don't call me aunt."

"Run along, Kate," said Helen. "You can see your aunt when she's dressed." She raised the shade, lowered the window, fluffed the curtains. Midmorning sun swallowed the room. Just like Helen to admire the acid glare of the morning sun. As a young girl, no matter how late Helen had been up the night before, she awoke at seven craving light and action, and splintering Virginia's last hours of sleep.

"Why can't I call you aunt?" Kate asked her.

"Can we be friends if I'm as old as an aunt? I never liked anybody I called aunt."

The child turned and walked through the doorway. Virginia had last seen her when she was not quite three, a silent shadow among the champagne drinkers at her wedding, so silent that Virginia had forgotten to bestow the promised last kiss as she and Julian departed. The child probably did not remember.

"She's plump through the backside," Virginia said as the door clicked shut.

"So were you at her age," said Helen, as if it were a matter of indifferent fact. She picked Virginia's scattered silks and laces from the floor and piled them on a small rose chintz chair.

Virginia got out of bed to look in the mirror. How firm can you be? "I was a compulsive eater," she said, "and then I decided I'd rather steal. Good thing, too. Julian likes the young boy look. Liked. I guess he still does. Remember how I used to steal everything I could get my hands on?"

"You're just talking," said Helen. Virginia thought her smile was a paper airplane zipping about the room.

"Once upon a time there was fifty cents missing," said Virginia, "just to refresh your memory. And the mommy and the daddy decided ad hoc which of two little girls took it and she was sent to her room until she would confess and long about three hours later she told a fat story about treating the neighborhood to sodas so that the mommy and the daddy would think she was generous if crooked."

Helen laughed in her throat. "You've still got your terrific imagination."

"A couple of weeks later I really did steal fifty cents but they never missed it. The depression must have lifted."

"A lot of children steal," said Helen. "Status. Kate used to steal. I was a long time finding out why."

"I bet you did, though," said Virginia.

"It was because the children were teasing her about her glasses."

"So now she's getting plump through the backside. Where'd she go? Kate! Hey, Kate!" Virginia called.

Kate walked in at once. She held her glasses in her hand and her eyes looked unfocused. Movie star eyes, Virginia thought, full of Murine and vagueness.

"You're the prettiest little girl I ever saw," Virginia said. "Let's you and me go to the zoo this afternoon."

"Aren't I too old for the zoo?" suggested Kate.

"At eight? I'll buy you a balloon."

"I know I'm too old for a balloon," said Kate with a large proud smile.

"And I know you're too young to be so funny," said Virginia, scruffing Kate's head.

"Don't go out today," said Helen, as if weighing the matter. "Warren won't be here and I thought we could have the day to ourselves."

"I didn't blame you for not saying you stole that fifty cents," said Virginia.

"What fifty cents?" asked Kate.

"Not you, baby. Your mother."

Helen put on a pleasant face and said, "Please, Virginia."

"Look, baby," said Virginia. "We'll go to the zoo tomorrow."

When Helen left the room to get Virginia a cup of coffee, the child remained. She put on her glasses and eyed Virginia. "Mother says you don't have a husband any more. Is he dead?"

"No. Well, yes, you might say that," said Virginia.

"And you don't have any children to remember him by?"

"No, I don't have any children to remember him by. All I have is eighteen hundred dollars a month."

"That's a lot of money," said Kate, looking impressed.

"Enough to remember somebody by," said Virginia.

"You talk funny," said Kate. "Are you really Mother's sister?"

"I believe it if you do," said Virginia.

She collected her things, off the rose chintz chair, off the fruitwood bureau, off the rose hookrug. Why had she come, she asked herself. As Julian said, on eighteen hundred dollars a month she could go anywhere, do anything. So why pretend that after five years of being guided by the expert hand of Julian to the best, the very best—La Femme in Paris and Casals at Prades, the Claridge hotels in every city and the febrile beauties of every sex—she could ever find what she wanted in a Chicago suburb with her sister patting her shoulder.

None of the recent past would make the least sense to Helen. She would say something embarrassing, like My but you have seen life. They had nothing in common except the shared early past. Women on the loose, Virginia thought, ought to stay that way. No chintz rooms and *à la recherche.*

This time last year exactly—March—was Bermuda. And it was lovely, peaceful, clean, until on the third day Julian had gotten his desperate look which meant he had found something worth prowling for. Every time the bar door swung open he had grinned anxiety all over. Virginia had felt like biting him.

"Dear Julian," she had said. "I wish I could be like you. I wish I could get myself in a frenzy every other week as you do."

"Don't be ugly," said Julian, in his smoothest voice. "You wouldn't like it a bit. It would destroy your charming *dégagé.*"

"Is that a noun?" asked Virginia.

"Those pearls look lovely on you," said Julian softly. "Absolutely translucent against that pink linen."

Virginia said nothing, fingering the pearls, his most recent gift. She had wanted them and she had gotten them and that was that. Under his gently mocking yet distracted gaze, she wished the door would swing open and the right person would come in, so they could both relax. Finally it did and before Julian could turn she said, "There he is." And Julian got that ripe red look.

That time had finished it except for the eighteen hundred a month and an occasional affectionate postcard sent through her lawyer. Next day he had flown to Jamaica for a week and she had felt laughter at her back and she did not feel grand or mysterious or even cold.

"Where've you been?" she asked Kate. "I've been to Bermuda."

"Nowhere," said Kate, answering an accusation. "What's Bermuda?"

"I'll take you there some day," said Virginia, "if you won't run off to Jamaica."

Virginia went in the bathroom, taking her clothes and cosmetics with her. She had removed her gown and put on her brassiere and slip when she heard a dull snap as if her suitcase had been unlocked. She cracked open the door and watched as the child peered into the side pockets of the suitcase, finally selecting a bracelet of sapphires which she attempted to fasten around her neck. Virginia opened the door wider and the child looked up. A complete innocent, Virginia thought. Children don't have enough expressions to choose the wrong one.

"What are you doing?" she demanded. No answer. Blank look. "Why are you meddling in my things?"

"I just am," said Kate without change of expression. "Are you going to tell Mother?"

"Maybe. What would she do if I did?"

"I guess not anything. Tell me I was tired," said Kate. "She says I act bad when I'm tired."

Virginia laughed. Helen the psychiatrist, ruining the child's justifications by substituting her own. "You're a regular monkey," she said. "How could Helen and Warren give birth to a monkey like you?"

"They just did," said Kate.

"Do they like each other?" asked Virginia. "Never mind, but you just stay out of my suitcase. You might find a skeleton or something."

"Of a monkey?" asked Kate, laughing, and Virginia was captivated.

Helen brought the coffee on a tray and it was hot and black. Chicory. Warren was from New Orleans so there was chicory, tasting like the continental coffee Virginia had persisted in hating. Warren was a plain man with strong appetites. Virginia had always thought his face was as public as a bulletin board. He walked to and from the train each day, staving off the coronaries. He read *Gods, Graves and Scholars* when it was *Gods, Graves and Scholars* and he read *The Lonely Crowd* when it was *The Lonely Crowd*. He had a tweed jacket with leather patches on the elbows. He did not seem to know that he was a plain man. But, she thought, at least you didn't have to look at his driver's license to know he was a man.

"What were you laughing about?" asked Helen, as if wanting to be glad if her daughter was amusing. "What did Kate do?"

Kate, looking out the window, showed an alert back. Virginia said, "Your daughter's a regular monkey. She can make faces just like a monkey. No wonder she doesn't want to go to the zoo."

"She never showed me," said Helen. She looked at Kate's back expectantly.

"You know how it is," said Virginia. "Mothers and daughters. I never showed Mother any of my monkeyshines either."

Kate turned around with a face that hadn't heard the conversation. She walked toward the door and when she got alongside Virginia, where her mother couldn't see, she drew down her chin, thrust out her lower teeth, and pretended to pick something from her head. Then she gave Virginia a dig in the hip. Virginia wanted to rub away a smudge she saw on the child's cheek but Kate walked on out of the room.

"She's cunning," said Virginia. "Very special."

"Yes, she is," said Helen. "I wish you'd had children. Then you wouldn't be quite so alone." At that, Virginia had a vision of ladies telling secrets, hungry ladies devouring morsels of sweets.

"I'm not alone, I'm young," she said. In spite of herself, she went on. "Children wouldn't have fit. Not with Julian, not with me."

"I always thought Julian would make a great father," said Helen.

Virginia eyed her. "You don't know what you're talking about."

It sounded too hard, a product not of the moment, which she had to admit was innocent, but of their old antagonism. And so she smiled placation.

"Of course I don't," Helen quickly said. "I only saw him at the wedding."

Typical Helen, Virginia thought, sailing in and out of squalls with a steady hand on the tiller. Little girl on father's knee cadging dimes with a kiss. Larger girl sharing non-secrets with a doting mother. Largest girl, dappled and clean, May bride all in white, with six pastel maids and six ushers and six groomsmen like the book said all in cutaways (rented) and gray gloves (gift of the groom) and a cutaway groom, plain Warren looking scrawny-necked. And why do even bull-like grooms look scrawny-necked?

And ten moderate years later, had the promise held? You bet your bottom dollar it had. Every last jot and tittle if you didn't count two miscarriages. The still lovely face scrubbed with Ivory, fingernails short and rounded, a house full of Baker and Dunbar (walk softly on my leather table), love, care, and beef Stroganoff, six hours a week for charity, Erich Fromm instead of Sunday, a cleaning woman twice a week, and baby-sitters galore. Galore. The whole thing was galore.

And yet, Helen got what she wanted too, the world she wanted wrapped in Christmas paper. She was moving along, singing her song. Why don't I like her? Virginia asked herself as she looked at Helen's open face. What's she done to me except be my sister all my life?

"It doesn't matter whether Julian would have been a good father or not," she said. "He won't now. Not to mine anyway." She thought that was a good joke and she laughed. For a crazy moment she thought she would tell Helen about Julian, but she decided not to. It would merely seem ugly to Helen. She would never comprehend the quid pro quo.

But the weakness had apparently been spotted, for Helen said, "Would you like to tell me about it? I always thought you had the world by the tail. You and Julian seemed to have everything, looks, brains, money. And now . . . nothing."

"Nothing?" repeated Virginia. "Don't forget the eighteen hundred a month. Can't call that exactly nothing."

Helen dismissed money. "What did happen? What went wrong?"

"Do you suppose," asked Virginia, "that I could have some breakfast?"

Hurt left Helen's face in shadows. Hastily she said, "I'm sure you're famished." She stood up and walked toward the door, then turned back with an embarrassed smile. "I don't mean to pry," she said, "but you are my sister and I do care."

"Bacon and eggs," said Virginia, "sunny side up."

By midafternoon, Virginia was mildly bored and irritated, slightly drunk on sherry, and she thought a little in love with the child. Every hour or so she was shown off like a new acquisition by Kate. One by one the children of the neighborhood were dragged in, silent little girls with their mouths ajar and eyes solemn. "That's my aunt," said Kate, "but I call her Virginia, not Aunt Virginia, because we're friends."

"I'm a museum piece," said Virginia, "en route to the Smithsonian."

"You're the most glamorous thing she's ever seen," said Helen. "If it bothers you . . ."

"I haven't had this much attention in years," said Virginia, "and it is something to do."

Helen looked uncomfortable. Their conversation had been crippled all day, stumbling and falling, tripped by Virginia, rescued by Helen. Virginia called herself perverse, and enjoyed it.

"When Warren comes home," said Helen, "we'll have a martini." It was presented like a promise to brighten the day and again Virginia felt the rise of malice.

"Won't he let you have the key?" she asked.

"Now really," Helen began, but an act of will captured indignation, and she smiled sisterly. "If you want one now, let's," she said. Virginia tapped her sherry glass, an indefinite gesture intended to leave Helen dangling, which it did.

At the window another small child peered in, not trusted by Kate to examine the acquisition save through glass. Virginia raised her sherry in a toast and winked. A hurried exchange outside the window followed and the child was brought in. After the ritual of identification, Kate said, "She wants to see your bracelet."

"Which one, baby?" asked Virginia.

"You know," said Kate.

"Would you like to run away with me and go to Europe and have lots of bracelets?" She turned to Helen. "That's a thought."

Kate looked at her friend. "Well," she said, doubtful.

"Don't then," said Virginia.

"Run along, Kate," said Helen. "Aunt Virginia and I are talking."

"Are we?"

"She talks funny," Kate said to her friend. She turned to Virginia and smiled in a very direct way. "Yes, I'd like to run away with you and have bracelets. I've never been to Europe."

"Come here, baby," said Virginia. But at a gesture from Helen the children departed to the upper regions of the house.

"Why couldn't she stay here?" asked Virginia. "Afraid I might say something she shouldn't hear?"

Helen laughed. "Call her back if you want to."

Virginia sipped her sherry, thought with distaste of a wine hangover. Thick and loggish. "I used to be able to get a quarrel out of you more easily than that," she said.

"You've been trying hard enough," said Helen abruptly. Her face showed release. "I'd hoped this time would be different, that we could be grown-ups instead of jealous little girls."

Virginia reached for the sherry bottle, banged it lightly against the tray's fence. It had been quite a long time since she had wished to attack anyone, or felt able to, and she felt ashamed and flushed and keen. "Two fingers only," she said, holding her fingers vertical.

"What's wrong, Virgie?" asked Helen.

Virginia drank solemnly. "No one's called me Virgie in a hundred years. Julian hated it. Sounds so bouncy." A few drops of sherry rained from the bottom of the glass onto her pale blue sweater. She waved off Helen's assistance.

"What's wrong, Virgie?" Helen repeated.

The name, the way it was spoken, reminded her of times, rare times, when there had been no quid pro quo, when it had seemed like two small girls against a towering world. Virginia felt the welling up of danger signals, of softness and pity, and she sat up straighter and cursed the sherry.

At once she decided to cut short her visit, send herself a telegram demanding her presence in New York, signed Julian, off somewhere God knew where with someone God knew whom. Final settlement, you know, so sorry to interrupt your lovely visit. The marvel of

Helen, heading God and herself both knew where with both knew whom, all holding hands, bored her, irritated her, made her shoulders ache. Dull and happy. Blonde and blue-eyed. Kate and her friend fled out the front door.

"I want a little air," said Virginia, wishing to follow them. "Sweet sherry is like being under a wet blanket. Steam. Let's go for a walk."

"I've got to put the roast in," said Helen. "In fifteen minutes or so?"

"In fifteen minutes I may not be able to find the exit. Where's Kate? Maybe she would walk with me."

Up in her room, Virginia put on a mustard-colored suede jacket, very country, dressing the part. She kept the old jacket as a reminder. It had been cleaned until the nap was slick smooth yet it still had the grease smudge on the cuff. A bicycle ride to the cemetery at Nice the day Maeterlinck was buried. Two months after her marriage, two days after her horrified discovery of Julian's tastes. A lovely young man had suggested the excursion, the intrusion, to pay respects, and she had grabbed it like a sword of vengeance. What had the young man looked like? A scrubbed cherry blonde? A languid candlelight brunette? She could not remember.

She did remember the prostrate widow dragged by two stalwart Belgians first in and then out of the small chapel. The young promise beside Virginia began to weep softly at the black figure in the brilliant sun glare, turning out to be Julian's young man, not her own at all. She had wheeled away in fury and self-pity and coasted back to their hotel by the sea. She had slipped on a spread of grease in a side street, fallen, greased her suede cuff, greased and cut her hands so that they bled red and black. She had had to steer the bicycle with the thumbs and index fingers of her hands, a gesture which finally struck her as a sublime caricature of all her troubles. By the time she got to the hotel she had felt the situation's full absurdity and she was laughing.

Her understanding with Julian, their happy quid pro quo, had dated from that soured revenge. They had not quarreled since. That night he had presented her with amethyst earrings, but she preferred the jacket.

On the sidewalk in front of Helen's Georgian house, Virginia called Kate. From three houses away came an answering shout and the child ran to her, looking questions. "I won't bite," said Virginia. "Come for a walk to the village."

A sign read, 55 CHILDREN PLAY ON THIS STREET — DRIVE CAREFULLY. A woman in bright plaid slacks was raking leaves and stopped to wave cheerily. Seven girls in brown beanies and with dull brown dresses hanging below their tan jackets walked past them and did not speak. Virginia noticed that Kate had on a tan jacket too.

"I don't want to be a Brownie," said Kate.

"I don't either," said Virginia.

Kate laughed. "You're too old."

"Don't be rude. Why not be a Brownie? I thought everybody wanted to be a Brownie."

"I just don't," said Kate.

"Because. Just because. You're a regular little female already." Virginia reached to take Kate's hand. "Don't worry about Brownies. They don't care about them in Europe. They think it's silly and so do I."

"I don't like those girls," said Kate. She caught her breath and plunged on. "There was this girl in my grade? And she had this pin and she gave it to me? And then she said she didn't and they said they were going to tell the teacher I stole it." Kate's shoulders rose to her ears and Virginia tightened her grip on the child's hand.

"But you didn't and you don't," she said. "I like you. I think you're about the most attractive little girl I know." They walked half a block in silence. Virginia said, "Your mother was a Brownie but I never was."

"Will you really take me to Europe?" asked Kate. Virginia nodded. Kate looked back over her shoulder. "Mother said if there's no room next year, she'll form a troop."

At one of the two drugstores of the village, Virginia ensconced Kate in a booth with a chocolate soda, while she went to the telegraph office.

"Must have you in New York Monday for final settlement.

Julian," she wrote. She scratched out Julian and wrote "Love, Julian." No hard feelings. She told the attendant, a large unkempt woman ruminating on a piece of clove gum, to telephone the message. The woman eyed her suspiciously.

Walking back to the drugstore, Virginia wondered where she would really go and quickly decided why not New York. Why lie? She wondered if her old friends would be as happy to see her alone. She decided probably not but they could stand it a couple of days. The one sure thing was that she didn't want to stay in this neat little village with her neat sister any longer. Nothing personal, only the everlasting differences between the abstractions. When she entered the drugstore Kate was wiping foam off the inside edge of the glass with her fingers.

Virginia put her hand on the child's neck and rubbed her thumb across the topmost vertebra. "I'll buy you a present," she said. "What?"

"You don't have to," said Kate, sucking her fingers. A shudder ran down her spine. "A dead man just walked over my grave."

Virginia cupped the child's skull in her hand and tried to think of a fine present. Only clothes came to mind. No jackets, no bermuda shorts, no little middle-class uniform. "All right, I won't buy you a present. I'll give you twenty dollars and you buy yourself one."

"That's a lot of money." Kate looked as if riches had been spread before her. "I'll buy Mother something."

"Look, baby," said Virginia as she pulled the child to her feet, "nobody's going to grade you."

Outside it was colder and growing dark. Virginia bundled Kate up, tying her own scarf around the child's neck. She held Kate's hand as they walked. Warm pudgy hand. Grimy and damp. Kate's other hand, rammed into the pocket of her coat, clutched the twenty-dollar bill.

Virginia thought about her own childhood and wondered if anyone had ever given her twenty dollars. Fifty cents, she remembered, from a drunken retired army major who smelled of stale beer. He was an old friend of her father's and he called her Toots. Or had he called Helen Toots? As usual her childhood stayed out of sharp focus. Save for a few intense brightly lighted recollections, her childhood was a vast impersonal landscape inhabited by two undifferentiated little girls. That's our memories, she thought. Not a tidy box of goodies to be dipped into, but only a particular sympathy for a shadowy child who like as not would turn out on further inspection to be Helen.

In front of the house, Kate stopped and asked, "Why did you give me twenty dollars?"

"I just did," said Virginia.

"Because. Just because," said Kate and they both laughed. "Don't forget to tell Mother you did." She ran off, calling out the names of children and waving the twenty-dollar bill like a captured flag. Virginia went in the house.

A fire of compressed sawdust was glowing and in front of it sat Helen, down cushions and a teacup. Virginia poured herself a glass of sherry and sat down with one leg tucked under her.

"We've been to the village," she said. "Kate and I." She paused a moment. "Do you mind my saying it's a dreadful place?"

"Yes," said Helen. "I do mind."

Virginia held the sherry before her eyes, watched the liquid dancing, and gradually formed an idea that had been inchoate all day. "But what about Kate?" she said. "All this is all right for you and Warren, but Kate's miserable here."

"Kate's just a child," said Helen.

"She hates it," said Virginia. "Anyway, one little two little three little Indians, all in jackets."

Helen laughed, with effort, looking drawn. "I suppose it's all in how you look at it."

"What if she went to school in Switzerland for a year or two?" Virginia shot out. "I'd look after her for you. In fact, it would give me something to do."

Nothing about Helen indicated she considered the idea. "You don't seem to understand we're a family."

"So you're going to make damn sure Kate grows up just like you. Warren works hard twenty-five years to earn twenty-five thousand so the proper dull finish can be put on Kate so she can marry a little

Warren and the next generation and the next. Teacups and down cushions." The day's irritations, or was it a lifetime's, came pouring out, and even as she spoke she felt how cruel though right, how unfair though just she was. "Kate's worth more than this, Helen, is all I mean," she finished, smiling brightly.

Helen's mask of patience broke and the threads of her clean face tightened into gulleys and ridges, a topography of anger.

"This may pass for sophisticated humor," she said, "but I'm afraid I don't find it very funny. I don't know what five years with that man has done to you, but this has been an extremely unpleasant day and . . ."

A little rocky on her feet, Virginia stood up. "I'll change for dinner and behave and be sorry and be sisterly. Shall we let bygones?"

Helen nodded, looking defensive and proud of her show of anger.

In her room, Virginia decided to be glamorous. She took off her sweater and skirt and put on a pale blue wool dress, simple and stunning. She went to her suitcase to get the sapphire bracelet and earrings. She found the earrings but not the bracelet. She looked through the suitcase, she looked in another one she hadn't opened since she had been there. She looked in the bathroom, under the bed, in the bed, in her suede jacket, in the pockets of her dressing gown. She even looked in her nightgown, which had no pockets.

When she went downstairs, she carried one large sapphire earring in each hand. She could not make up her mind what to do. She put both earrings in one hand and poured herself a glass of sherry. She wondered if she would be sick from all the sherry. Helen walked in from the kitchen.

"Don't you look pretty," said Helen, patting her own rumpled skirt. She glanced into a bright silver ashtray and pulled a stray lock of hair behind her ear. She looked at Virginia's hand. "What's that?" she asked.

"Sherry," said Virginia, biding her time.

"Sapphire earrings," said Helen. "Aren't they lovely."

"Because of a young Sicilian," said Virginia.

"What?"

"The bracelet's gone."

Helen reacted at once. "Not since you've been here," she declared. When Virginia nodded, Helen laughed, looked quickly around the room, frowned. Her face looked dirty. "Have you looked everywhere?"

"I don't think you took it," said Virginia.

"Kate." Helen sat down abruptly. She unbuttoned the top button of her blouse. She looked drenched.

"Never mind," said Virginia. "She won't hock it."

Helen stared at her. When she spoke her voice was sober and cold. "I hope you're satisfied. You've been hoping for something like this all day, though God knows why. All that talk of bracelets and Europe. I hope you're satisfied!"

"Why try to blame me?" asked Virginia. "You said yourself she stole."

Helen rubbed her fingers over her lips, smearing lipstick. "That was a long time ago. A year next month. We had it licked. Until you came."

"Once a thief . . ." said Virginia. The words hung in the air, attracting flies. Virginia wished she could withdraw them, cancel out the deadeye strike of her betrayal.

"Thief," Helen repeated.

They stared across the room at each other, half listening, after twenty years, for the heavy voice of authority to force them to pretend a love they didn't feel, to return what had been taken, to give what had not been offered, to speak more kindly. Kate walked in, flushed with cold and smiling.

"Hi, Virginia," she said.

"Kate," said Helen.

"Come here, baby," Virginia said.

Kate looked from one to the other, opened her mouth and lowered her chin and began to pant softly.

"Come here, baby," Virginia said again.

"Stay out of this," said Helen. "It's no business of yours."

"It's my bracelet."

"It's my child," said Helen.

"What bracelet?" asked Kate. She wiped her arm across her face, leaving damp smears of dirt.

"She hasn't got it," said Virginia. "Have you, baby?" She smiled at Kate, nodded, held out her arms, nodded again.

"Please, Virginia," said Helen. "Kate, I want you to tell me where the bracelet is. No questions, no punishment. Where is it?"

Kate made a sudden choice, ran to Virginia and let herself be folded in the waiting arms. "You don't trust me, you think I steal," she screamed.

Hugging Kate to her, Virginia felt the hard unmistakable outline of the bracelet on the child's upper arm, not visible to the eye but distinct to the touch. Kate slumped boneless against her.

"She hasn't got the bracelet," said Virginia. "I have it."

"It's too late for that."

"In my suitcase. Right-hand zipper pocket. Look for yourself."

"Kate," said Helen.

"Lord!" shouted Virginia. "It was a joke, just a joke!"

"Joke," repeated Helen. Her face looked torn down the middle, hope and doubt quarreling through her.

Virginia put her hand on the child's warm neck flesh, felt the dead man's shudder roll down her spine. "It's all right, baby, it's all right," she whispered.

The insistent shrill of the telephone split the room and after looking desperately from Kate to Virginia, Helen walked out of the room to answer it.

Virginia kissed the child, hugged her, reached inside her coat, undid the bracelet, dropped it in the pocket of her dress, and said, "You're my little monkey."

"It's for you," said Helen at the doorway. Virginia released the child and went to the telephone. Western Union told her she was wanted in New York. Love, Julian. As she re-entered the living room she heard Kate say, "I wasn't stealing it, I don't do that any more. I was showing it to the kids. I didn't think she'd mind. But then I got scared."

"It's all right," said Helen, "it's all right." She rocked Kate in her arms.

Two heads on one body, they looked up as Virginia approached. Clean faces washed by the same tears. Virginia felt three rooms away, bare rooms without rugs. The stranger three rooms away. She took the bracelet from her pocket and snapped it on her wrist. Blue on blue. Shine on dull.

"Wrong number," she said.

Jangling her bracelet as she poured herself just a splash of sherry, she looked from one to the other and laughed.

"Wrong number," she repeated, barely able to get the words out. She thought she had never heard anything quite so ludicrous, quite so funny in all her life.

Front Man in Line

"Dapper Dan, the ladies' man, here comes your boyfriend, Miriam, here comes your boyfriend ugh." That was Sherry Wilkins, not quite twenty, still supporting (it gave Miriam pleasure to note) that hill country Baptist preacher voice that was the perfect vehicle, God-made, for reprimand and outrage. Oh, if you turned around to see her, you saw certain natural and undeniable attractions encased in what you could not distinguish from any Hollywood tart. That unbeatable combination of being young, glamorous, and right.

But why should Miriam waste her moments, her nerves vilifying the girl? Because Miriam was deeply implicated and it sickened her. For, indeed, there he did come, Dapper Dan, the ladies' man, straight at Miriam, his destination, his destiny as he sometimes said.

Helped to the curb by the chauffeur, his powder-blue, pouter-pigeon wife issuing last-minute cautions from the back seat, he dragged along behind his silver-headed cane, frail and salacious. He was gallant, wanton, and over eighty. His black shoes, his cream suit, his vast pearl stickpin, his lifeless wisps of yellowed hair floating in the breeze were advertisement of him. He fairly glistened, inside and out. He considered himself a rake. Nearly everyone else considered him a bother and an old fool. However, he was Daniel Shirer, Dapper Dan Shirer, and his name rang like a cash register in the city. No one swept him off the doorstep when he made his biweekly pilgrimage to his money.

Miriam Labadie, born Sims in better days and now forty-six, a widow, a receptionist-stenographer in an investment house, was never caught napping by the old reprobate, although he tried to sneak in noiselessly to steal a free pat on her arm. Always she heard his cane tip-tapping along the vinyl floor, and she turned before he could touch her. The office manager accepted the old man's attentions to her and pretended to think that Miriam deserved the credit for the old man's account. The girl, Sherry Wilkins, accepted nothing, pretended nothing, credited no one.

Miriam wished the old man would forget her, devil take the firm. It was a biweekly ordeal a fastidious woman ought not to endure. She tried to be distant and courteous, but her smiles felt like trapped dying mice. Her most casual good-mornings were assumed by him to be offerings, seductions. Mr. Shirer's hand, raised, seemed to ache to pat her on the bottom. Sometimes her hand ached to slap his hand; sometimes, God help her, her bottom ached to be patted. Time and circumstance had reduced Daniel Shirer to this and her to Daniel Shirer. Imminent humiliation dampened her spirits. She liked the old man.

She kept at her typewriter until he was almost upon her. Cat and mouse, but she didn't want that hand plying at her flesh. And yet she was, and admitted it, still coquette enough to be glad to see a bit of expectancy rise on a man's face, even that man's. She saved herself from his touch at the last moment, came swiveling around to face him across the mahogany railing.

"Why, Mr. Shirer," she said, "I was afraid you weren't coming."

"Am I late? Am I late?" Distracted, he hauled from his watch pocket a giant gold timepiece, as old as himself, and peered through faded eyes at its faded face. He loathed being late on his rounds about the city. He had once confided in her: I'm rich for being on time, I'm watching the old ticker tape while the slugabeds are going broke.

"Right on the button as always," she said. "I set my watch by you."

"Time is money," he said. And then something—a visceral ticking, a pain in his leg, the skipping of a heartbeat—brought him back to what was now more important than time and money. His eyes glinted. Lust, Miriam thought, he can't stay off it. "I've brought you something," he said, jerking his shoulder to indicate the hand held behind his back. Another stolen offering, she thought, but before she could pretend any interest, the young righteous voice behind her said, "Mr. O'Neal said when and *if* you get free, Miriam."

Shirer stepped back as if someone had shoved him. "I'm keeping you," he said, sagging. "You'd rather be doing something else."

Forget her, Miriam wanted to say, she's just young. "Rather work than talk to you? Never," she answered, giving him her very kind smile. He stared at her, wanting more. She gave more. "I'd rather talk to you than most anything."

"Ah now, Mrs. Labadie, most anything?" he said quite quickly, leering at her, as sly as a rat, a nasty old man once again.

Surely he was more than that. Something had guided him safely over the eighty years to here. Intelligence, they said, not just money-shrewd but real intelligence, a moderate man, quite the gentleman, reserved like his time, but, they said as sadly they shook their heads, he just didn't have time to get done with his skirt-chasing. Of course not, Miriam thought ruefully, save the skirt-chasing until too late and inappropriate, and then, even then, direct it at a middle-aged woman who was insulted and grateful.

And with that thought, she felt compelled to remove herself from him, to show that she was not conniving with him and, God forbid, enjoying his advances. "I do have work to do," she said.

"Did I offend you?" he asked, in bewildered innocence. "I didn't go to do it. Why would an old codger like me ever offend a pretty young lady like yourself?" He gleamed at his words and eagerly pressed the advantage he thought he had gained. "Why if I got paid I don't think I could, it'd be asking too much of an old man who thinks as highly of you as I do. You know I think highly of you, don't you?" His gaze pinched her and he waited for an answer.

"I know," she said, and she did, and she was ashamed of herself for the anger, slight as it was, and she was angry with everyone. She flashed him her middle-aged gaiety smile, and pointed at his concealed hand. Get on with it, hand me the withered chrysanthemums you snitched from your wife's centerpiece. But this time it wasn't flowers.

"This is for you," he said, holding forth a two-pound box of candy. His grand proud gesture justified a diamond of equal size. "All chocolate, every one of them chocolate. Didn't you say any flavor was all right just so long as it was chocolate?"

"I did," she said, "I made that clever remark." He missed that and she was glad. Always, it seemed, she had a smart-aleck comment and always she regretted it. The box had no cellophane wrapping, which he instantly became aware of.

"I took the cover off, to be sure it was chocolate," he explained. "Can't trust the merchants these days."

She knew he had not bought it but merely slipped it out from home. He never really bought her anything, apparently he was too close-fisted for that. Instead, he robbed his own or his wife's possessions and brought Miriam the loot. And what a sorry loot it usually was.

Once he had brought her a little silver bonbon dish, slightly tarnished, wrapped in a wrinkled grocery sack and tied with string. Written across the sack in his large bold quavering hand was: To Miriam Labadie with highest esteem, from her no longer secret admirer. Feeling foolish and disloyal, Miriam telephoned his wife, herself approaching eighty but no less formidable for that, and reported the gift which she then sent out by the firm's messenger. From then on she had known where the withered flowers and the half-eaten boxes of candy and the yellowing handkerchiefs came from, but she did not betray him again. She did not want to hear his wife again say, "He's gotten a little senile is why he bothers you." "Oh we all just love him," said Miriam. "He doesn't bother me."

And who knew, really, if there was more bother than pleasure in his gallant attentions? Not Miriam Labadie, alone in her apartment, arranging withered flowers, tasting stale chocolates, and laughing to herself over her crazy senile gallant old and only beau, God help her.

As she opened the box and dug among the candies, avidly he watched her, and as he watched he raised his hand toward and above her. She feared that hand coming down on her, her shoulder, her breast, seeking payment for the candy she accepted only out of kindness. She pushed herself from the railing and Mr. Shirer's hand fell back upon himself, fingering his pearl stickpin, and the disappointment on his face turned to confusion. She had seen it happen before. Thwarted, he seemed to lose direction and become helpless, an old man no longer dapper, merely pitiful.

"Let me call Mr. O'Neal for you," she said, placing him. "You want Mr. O'Neal now, don't you?"

"I want you," he said. His intention reformed and he stayed her with a gesture. Slyly he finished, "for a bit of lunch perhaps?" His hands, palms toward her, begged her to be gentle for he was at her mercy. No harm meant, he seemed to say, and yet his demands, his desires, grew each week, as if fed on her refusals. A walk to the bus stop, or coffee, a ride home with him and his chauffeur, and now lunch. What would it be next time? Would he finally march in and say Let's go to bed?

"If you keep bringing me candy like this I'll never be able to eat lunch again."

Usually he accepted defeat gracefully, as if even a No from her was pleasure.

"I won't be bringing you candy much longer," he said. He gazed around the room and spoke, not directly to her, but more to himself, in a very private voice.

"I'm sorry you feel that way about it, Mr. Shirer," said Miriam. "I always lunch with the other girls and . . ."

"I'll be dead," he said, "I won't be in this race much longer." His expression was vague and unfocused and his voice was self-pitying and begging pity. But to acknowledge that was to involve herself more deeply, which she resented very much. She said, in an airy casual voice, "What a thing to say. Your kind lasts forever, you'll be here long after the rest of us are gone."

Empty, idle, lying words, but he liked them. Perceptibly he brightened, straightened, tightened. His hand rose toward her and as it did she had a vision.

A long long endlessly long chain of bedraggled people, walking without rhythm and out of step, more like a fleeing mass than an army. She saw herself somewhere near the middle, rather tall and erect and staring and perhaps set apart just a little. The mass thinned out toward the front, looked worn and old and exhausted, walked in staggers, barely upright, as dry as winter trees. And out in front of all, a high step or two ahead, was Daniel Shirer, going on and on and on, jaunty as he staggered, lustful, pursuing, eager, his raised searching hand falling back upon his pearl stickpin and then rising again and again and again.

"You're the leader of the whole band of us," she said. "What would we do without you?"

"I like to hear you say that," he said, as grateful as a child. He reached to touch her hand, so gently that she did not move it. "You've got a way with you a man likes, Mrs. Labadie. I talk with you and by God I decide maybe I'll just live forever. You stay as pretty and sweet as you are and they'll have to send down a brigade of armed angels to get me. Yessir, at least a brigade." His hand went to her wrist and she said, withdrawing her hand, "I'll lose my job if I don't get to work. You better go see Mr. O'Neal."

"Quite right," he said. Out came the gold watch and off he dragged. Just before disappearing into O'Neal's office, he cocked his head back to Miriam. "I'll be back for a little piece of chocolate, though."

"He means a little piece of you," said Sherry Wilkins. "I just wouldn't put up with that. I just wouldn't."

Miriam did not respond. Twice a week she had to endure the two of them, the wheedling of the old, the contempt of the young. Did they quarrel through her? When she turned back to her work, letters announcing the purchase of this, the sale of that, she could not concentrate. She was not exactly ruffled, but she had felt a flutter of sensitivity with the old man, as if unwanted feeling had almost surfaced. And yet she was accustomed to the old man and their ritual of tease and flirtation and titillation and rejection. That was hardly new.

Pretty and sweet he had called her. Was that it? And she had called him the leader of the band. She saw him that way, the leader, the front man, the oldest man she knew, it was no lie. Nor, by the same token, had he done more than say for that moment what he saw. He had laid no claim to immortal truth. He merely saw her pretty and sweet, instead of forty-six and atrophied in widowhood and lonely. Sweet, yes, perhaps. Perhaps even pretty. A little. Still. Still a little pretty. Miriam thought that she would like to wash her hands where he had touched her.

"I think I'll wash my hands," she announced to no one.

"I don't blame you," said Sherry.

"Oh hush," said Miriam. "Leave him be, he's just a harmless old man." She sat back down.

"Dirty old man, I think they call it. Honestly, Miriam, you just ask for it. Not that you asked me but in my experience a man . . ."

"What experience?" asked Miriam.

"What?"

"A nineteen-year-old Romeo? Some thirty-year-old sophisticate you wrestled best two out of three in the back seat of a taxi? Or your grandfather, that dirty old man?"

"I never claimed . . ."

"You're young," said Miriam. "You don't know anything. You have no idea what it means to be nearly fifty and alone."

"Fifty? Why he hasn't been anywheres near fifty in over thirty years." She paused, ignored her stupidity, prissed her lips and prepared her face for a venture into wit. "In thirty years the nearest he's been to fifty is trying to put his hands all over you."

"I'm nearly fifty," said Miriam. She felt she wore the soiled look of an old and lascivious woman.

"Oh you," said the girl, forgiving the quarrel. Her smile condescended to the difference between them.

Carrying with her the damaged image of herself, Miriam turned away. Did the girl not hear the whisperings of time and circumstance? Apple breasts she had, high on a stiff proud body, and a firm ungirdled untouched bottom. Hands off, everybody. And not from prudery or a desire to barter, but from arrogance and ignorance, as if what counted was the body and the hand, objects, without meaning until there was a touch between. A murky, smeared, and far-distant picture flicked in Miriam's fantasy—hinting sex between herself and Daniel Shirer—and was thrust away instantly, violent, so that seconds later she would have sworn she had not seen it.

Not fifteen minutes had passed when Shirer came out of Mr. O'Neal's office, with alacrity, as if sprung from jail, aiming right for her. Miriam thought that none of the men of her generation, surely not a younger one, would ever know how to flatter a woman with an approach like that, shy, eager, gallant, his expression begging sufferance. Miriam was preparing to give him back a little appreciation and welcome when a sound like a snort-sneer came from the girl. Miriam looked down at her typewriter. I live in this office, in this world, Dapper Dan, she said very distinctly to herself, with the likes of her, leave me alone, Dapper Dan, pass me by with barely a nod.

"Why, Mr. Shirer, back so soon?" she said.

"Soon? Why, time's winged chariot just won't move when I'm away from you, Mrs. Labadie." He grinned at her expectantly, demanding a response.

"You have world enough and time," she said.

"Ah, Miriam," he said, chewing on her name, tasting it in his mouth, and inviting her to invite him to use it. "Miriam, Miriam, a fine old name. They don't seem to use the good ones any more. Candace O'Brien, Sharon Cohen, Michele Jones, names that don't mean a thing any more. But then the young ones don't amount to much either, never will be the woman you are, Miriam, Mrs. Labadie. You're a real woman and they're just the rouge and perfume they wear, that's all."

Miriam enjoyed the discomfort that would cause the girl behind her, and momentarily she wondered if the old man had been deliberately mean. But she knew what he was really doing, persuading her to let him enjoy the intimacy of her given name.

"What's your wife's name?" she asked, like a foolish young girl on guard against the blandishments of married men. She felt so silly.

"Ruth," he said with a dismissing wave of his hand. He looked shrewd. "Which reminds me, she's been after me to get you to take supper with us one night real soon. How does that strike you?"

"I don't even know your wife," said Miriam.

"She knows you, though. You think I don't talk about you at home?" He smirked a bit and leaned closer to her. "Why, you won't believe it but she's a jealous woman, as old as we are, and it's you got her going these days." He stepped back to see his effect.

"How perfectly foolish," said Miriam, and she meant it two ways, the social disclaimer and the deep disgust.

"I wouldn't say that," said Mr. Shirer. He came again to the railing and leaned across, balanced so precariously at his belt that Miriam was afraid his legs would fly up and she'd have him in her lap. He whispered, "She's not much wife to me these days and she knows it."

His breath, metallic and stale with dentures and age, flowed over her and she drew back. "I won't tolerate that kind of talk," she said. With the flush rising through her neck, she whipped her chair around and commenced to pick at the typewriter. She saw from the outside range of her vision that Mr. Shirer had slumped, barely upright, against the railing with his head abjectly on his chest.

"I don't know why I say things like that," he said. "I don't mean to offend you. What is it happens to a man that he goes around insulting young ladies? And we do, almost all us old men do. Is it a way of proving we're alive?"

His face was as intelligent and moderate, as focused and thoughtful, as she was sure it had been in his good years. Miriam felt awkward and indecisive and she was torn between wanting to comfort and forgive him and wanting to use this for a final break with him.

"Mr. O'Neal just rang for you," said the voice behind her, condescending again, saving Miriam from her own weakness. In a stroke of outrage and pride, Miriam swung toward the voice.

"O'Neal can wait," she said, "and you too." The young face, pretty, righteous, and petty, filled her with rage. What good were the young to her, she had lost them long ago. "You just mind that little self of yours, you hear?"

She swiveled back to Mr. Shirer, expecting to see that his spirits had ascended on the power of her words, her acceptance of him. Apparently they had not registered on him, for he looked whipped and thoughtful, musing on himself.

"First you forget the names," he said. "Then you forget the faces. Then you forget to button your pants, and then you forget to unbutton them. That has happened to me. And some place along the line you want the young women, you begin dreaming of the young women. To keep you alive, I guess. Like Solomon."

"None of that," said Miriam, cheery and coy. "I won't have that talk from a gallant old . . . buzzard like you. Why, it's a reflection on me, don't you see, a terrible reflection. If it's only because you're old, then it's not because I'm . . . well, because I'm what I hope I am anyway."

His smile was bleak, knowing, self-pitying. She recognized her failure and she rose from her chair and leaned across the railing to pull him closer to her. She pecked at his cheek with her lips.

"I never did thank you for the chocolates," she said. She thought she had done quite a nice thing and she was annoyed when his nod of gratitude was perfunctory.

"They were my wife's," he said. "I look generous at her expense. Your expense. Her expense. At my age you stay alive at somebody else's expense. If I were God I wouldn't let us."

You just keep on staying alive, she wanted to say to him. She sought for a clue, a better word, a gesture to redeem the moment. Calculations and plans flashed through her mind, inane, pointless, selfish, as perfunctory as her kissing gift had been, and as doomed to failure. She watched him slowly dying before her eyes. And, helpless, at last instinct happened to her and in its darkness she went unerringly to her own inviting and submissive heart, and thus to his.

"If I were your wife, I'd feed you chocolates all day long and at night I'd just eat you up."

She thought someone else had spoken the words, their echo sounded so abandoned and shameless. Miriam Labadie? Never. But his face shifted toward lust and longing again and she knew that she had served him well. With malice he appraised her, and as he pressed across the railing, her instinct guttered and she was her prim proud self again. But she determined to be staunch. The instant before she closed her eyes she saw his hand flick out like a claw, willful and greedy. In her deliberate blindness, she felt his squeezing pat on her thigh.

When seconds later she opened her eyes, he was already departing, a look on his face of triumph and dominance and liberty and lust.

"See you Thursday," said Miriam. He glanced back and winked at her and that wink promised more more more. His need was insatiable, but so too was her own. She hoped he would live forever.

Outside the door, one hand grasping his cane, the other fingering his pearl stickpin, he joined the mass of people moving by her window. He was frail and jaunty and dapper and alive. Gaily she waved her hand for all her world to see. Pretty and sweet she felt, and safe for the time. Intently she watched him until he was out of sight.

Shadow of an Eagle

After living away from New York for nine years, Charley and Helen Osborn finally decided to go back for a visit. They arrived late on a cold night, made good on their reservation at a pleasant family-type hotel right off Madison, and went to bed. Not once in all the weeks of planning had they mentioned what was uppermost in their thoughts: Charley's brother Harry and his wife Martha.

Any mention of Harry made Helen furious and Charley very nervous. She still had raw wounds, and she prided herself on being a person not accidentally wounded. And Charley was a man who hated any kind of trouble and would avoid it at any cost to himself.

At the beginning of their marriage, Charley had tried to talk with Helen about Harry, to get him in a proper perspective for both of them. But if he so much as said, "Once, when Harry and I were kids . . ." Helen would come up with an angry smart remark like "And you were throwing his paper route so he let you read the funnies free of charge." Charley would stare at the wall and Helen would stare at him and Charley would finish the story to himself. Not at all, he would say, it wasn't that way at all. In fact . . .

On the third morning in New York, while they were having a late breakfast in the hotel dining room, and without actually having determined in advance to do so, Charley blurted it out.

"What I think I'll do today is call Harry."

"Do as you like." Helen's response shot out even before he had finished his sentence. She forced a cheerful, uncommitted look which

Charley took to mean that she was trying but not to trust her.

"Say what you think," said Charley. "You're in it, too. Suppose I call and suppose they invite us for dinner or drinks or something?"

"You think those two would take a chance on us for anything as precarious as eating or drinking?" asked Helen.

Charley decided not to be hurt or angry with her; he decided to be reasonable, patient, and successful. "Blood ties are blood ties," he said. "People would sure think it was funny if we didn't even call them."

"I never begrudge anybody a laugh," said Helen.

Charley knew that he had no chance in a scrap with her. While emotion made him nervous and silent, it made her quick and noisy. In that, she was like Harry. But, he thought, if silence, avoiding trouble, was a good trait as Helen said it was, then didn't he owe Harry something after all? Charley looked at the distant wall and said nothing and waited for the apologetic jest that was Helen's usual compromise.

She spread her hands, surrendering her hard resistance. "I'm just jealous," she said. "I'm a plain city-bred country woman and I never could compete with the likes of Martha. I'm all thumbs and left arms."

Charley moved right in. He laughed quickly and said, "I better call him before he gets away for lunch."

Going up in the elevator, Charley thought, a little ruefully, that if he had more character he would probably have as much resentment as Helen did. She was a rock and he was sand. When they had been courting, Helen had got quite a freeze from Harry and Martha—perhaps because she was awkward and uneasy with strangers and a little strong-minded with friends. Or perhaps because her family, in Queens, had put all the food on the table the night Harry and Martha were invited for dinner. (What a splendid meal, Martha had said. I hope I don't ruin any of these splendid dishes with my elbow.)

Harry, later, being intensely affectionate with a vise of fingers on Charley's knee, explained it in his succinct way: She won't help you one bit, Charley boy, with the people who count, and you are going to need help to make it big in this world. I don't particularly want to make it big, said Charley; you make it big for both of us. All right, all right, said Harry, his face flaming, forget I mentioned it, forget I give a good goddamn what happens to you. And the freeze was on.

Within two years of his marriage, and over Harry's strong objection, Charley sold Harry his half-interest in the brothers' fruit brokerage business. Helen pointed out that the "strong objection" had not been accompanied by an equally strong generosity, but Charley was satisfied that he had got his due. It was, after all, and Charley knew it, Harry who had built the business up from the two-truck peddling operation their father had left them.

Charley and Helen had gone to Texas to grow pink grapefruit. They had had a fine life. They spent three weeks each year in Mexico City, and Charley often found himself looking around the lobby of the Reforma to see if maybe Harry was there. At Christmas time, Charley selected a carefully nondescript card and on it he wrote a long note to Harry and Martha. Martha sent them a white card on which was written in embossed red, Seasons Greetings Martha and Harry Osborn parenthesis in Martha's hand *Why don't you ever ever come to New York* end of parenthesis. Second parenthesis, in Harry's flamboyant scrawl, *I miss you Charley Boy*. Also, two years back, Charley and Helen had received an invitation to the wedding of Harry's daughter Eve.

Charley moved his hat and gray topcoat to a chair and sat down on the moss-green, heavily corded bedspread. He looked up the telephone number of Osborn Fruit Brokerage, gave it to the operator, and waited nervously.

Always, Harry had made him feel shabby and awkward, as if his jacket was too large and his shirt collar too small. Harry was forceful and vain. Harry had a knack for making jokes and money and women. Harry was noticed, because of the vigor of his wide-legged stance, because of his shouting laughter, because he wanted to be noticed.

When they were boys, Charley had tried to be a little Harry. He had affected the way Harry let his knickers fall halfway down his leg. He showboated in basketball, and fouled out. Grown, he drank gimlets and hated gin. He let Harry get him into an athletic club and he went devotedly and swam and drank alone. He put the make on the most inaccessible belles and listened across the *sole véronique* as they confessed their passion for Shetland sweaters and Oreos. But at twenty-six he finally decided to give Harry up. He refused to be the eleventh person at dinner, the fifth man on the golf course, Harry's best audience, convenience, and friend. Finally, on a lonely Sunday afternoon riding on the top of a Fifth Avenue bus, he met Helen, fell in love, married her within two months, and relaxed. He read three newspapers every day, and took up, in order, cameras, star-gazing, hi-fi, and Indian lore, not one of which, he was pleased to note, would have interested his brother in the least.

When the telephone began to ring on the other end and the insistent jangling seemed to bring Harry closer, Charley thought with sudden full pride that the years had fortified him so that now, surely, he would view Harry in proper size.

A slight female voice answered and Charley asked to speak to Mr. Osborn. The pause was long, and just as he started to repeat his request the girl said Wait a minute. Charley waited and a man's voice, soft, drawling, came through. Charley asked again for Mr. Osborn.

"Who is this?" asked the man.

"Charley Osborn. Who is that?"

"I reckon I'm your nephew. I'm Bill Spencer."

"My nephew?" Helen walked in and he motioned her for a cigarette. Of course. Spencer was Eve's husband. Charley had sent twelve silver goblets.

"Didn't you get the wire?" asked Spencer. "Harry died of a heart attack yesterday morning, driving to the office, hit another car, almost killed . . ."

Heart attack, Charley thought. Heart attack Harry. Hairbreadth Harry. It was right: fast, painful, in the act of something, twisting a Rolls or a Porsche through angry traffic. He dropped the telephone in its cradle and closed his eyes. He felt a quick hard pain in his chest, felt it spread to his armpits, and he had a sense of floating and darkness. He opened his eyes and sat up on the edge of the bed.

"Harry's dead."

"What?" said Helen.

"Yesterday. Only yesterday. We might have seen him." The bed went down with Helen's weight and her arm dropped across his shoulder and rocked it back and forth.

"I'm sorry," she said. "I'm so sorry."

That hit Charley as false and wrong and he dropped his shoulder so that her arm slid off. "Don't counterfeit," he said. "You're just sorry because somebody, anybody, died. Not because Harry."

"Because your brother," she said.

"What kind of being sorry is that?" asked Charley. "I'm not crying, am I? Except at least I used to care. Never mind."

"I'm not a fool," said Helen. "I know what you mean."

"Take it easy," said Charley, as much to himself as to her. "I mean, forget us. Martha and Eve."

Driving to Texas, he and Helen had stopped to see Eve at her boarding school. When they told her they were leaving for good, she said Goddamn, goddamn, goddamn. Charley said, Is that what they teach you at expensive boarding schools? Yes, she said. Goddamn.

Within seconds, Charley thought, the dead—even the vibrant dead like Harry—recede and the living take over the stage. And that was the way it should be, let the dead.

"Are you going over?" asked Helen.

He nodded. "You?"

"If I can't even say I'm sorry to you, I guess I can't say it to them. I'll go to the funeral."

"That's big," said Charley. He did not understand why he wanted to challenge her, but he did.

"Are you quite suddenly furious because I came between you and Harry? Is that really honest?"

"Came between?" said Charley. "I thought you were supposed to have saved me from him." Before Helen could fuel up her fury, he turned on her a woeful face and shook his head. He got up and reached for his topcoat and hat.

"I'll be here," said Helen. "I'll read a book and if I'm not in the room I'll be down in the dining room. Just because we have breakfast at lunch time doesn't mean I ought to get gypped out of lunch, does it?"

"No," said Charley, and he turned away from her disappointed face.

As he sat in the back of the taxi, he wondered if Harry had made the *Times* obituaries. It would be a mark of distinction he would have wanted. The death of Will Harry Osborn occurred yesterday. Will Harry Osborn? With a name like that, Harry said when he was twenty-three, you're scratched before the race begins. He had tried several. William Harry Osborn. Harry William Osborn. Harry Williamson Osborn.

He had settled on Harry Williamson Osborn. What Williamson is that? asked Martha's friends. What Williamson could it be? Charley held his breath. Pure Oil, said Harry, straight as a die. The Pure Oil Williamsons. Except one fruity guy once said, I know of no Williamsons connected with Pure Oil. My mistake, said Harry, not Pure Oil, it was Pure Crap, we're part of the Pure Crap Williamsons, aren't we, Charley boy? And Harry laughed and laughed and laughed. Charley had had the distinct and admiring thought that all along Harry had said Pure Oil just so that one day he could say Pure Crap, and laugh. They'll never catch us, Charley boy, Harry had said. I'm dancing off before they know what hit 'em. Charley had said, They're not trying to catch me. Jesus, said Harry.

The apartment was in the middle eighties, an imposing structure alternating slices of bronze glass with slabs of white stone in an astigmatic checkerboard. The November wind was sharper than midtown, and as Charley got out of the taxi his hat, which he wore on the back of his head to protect his neck from the Texas sun, whipped off and rolled like a lame wagon down the street. The doorman retrieved it.

Charley told the doorman he was Mr. Osborn's brother and never mind announcing him. The doorman said to take the right-hand elevator which opened on the Osborns' half of the seventh floor.

The apartment door was right in front of the elevator. Charley pressed a small white button, and muted chimes sounded. After a moment the door was opened and there was Martha.

"Charley," she cried, in a gay girl's voice. He remembered that once Helen had said that the joke that voice was still laughing at was about You. Actually, he thought, it was a very nice voice.

She reached up and put her arms around his neck and kissed him. He felt pleased and a little emotional and young. He held her away from him to look at her. A streak of gray cut from her widow's peak to the crown of her head. Her hair was fine and glossy and black. Her hands, resting in his, were as white and delicate as lace. She was exquisite and delicate and white in her soft navy wool dress. Charley thought that his memory of her—lovely face like a sheathed knife (were those Helen's words?)—had been badly distorted. He wondered if the same thing had happened to his memory of Harry. He felt himself sag a little as he realized he would never know.

"I was so sorry, Martha," he said, "so very sorry. You and Eve."

"Thank you," she said, quietly, shaking her head. "Naturally, we were all . . ." She threw her hands in the air, as if helpless. "Where's Helen?"

Charley was caught off by the abrupt change, and he was annoyed with Helen. He couldn't invent a good excuse and he said, "Helen?" stupidly.

"You're not divorced, are you?"

The words slapped Charley and more testily than he intended he answered, "We're not even slightly divorced."

Martha laughed. "That's a grand way of putting it. So many people are slightly divorced. Harry and I right after the war, remember? I think we ought to be honest about these things right from the start. It wasn't perfect, after all. Harry was . . . well, Hairbreadth Harry as you used to call him, and I am inevitably I, and I won't pretend otherwise now. I'm not going to build up a great fantasy."

"The truth never hurts," said Charley. "I guess."

Martha tugged gently at his sleeve and drew him into the apartment. The conversation in the living room stopped when they entered, and everyone looked at him. There were two women and a man, and the man stood and said he was Bill Spencer, I beat you here after all, and Charley shook his hand.

The two women smiled, one crossed her legs a different way and the other, the younger one, reached for her glass on the low marble cocktail table. Charley realized the younger one was his niece, Eve, but he hesitated to recognize her. She was beautiful, a glowing beauty, and he wasn't sure how he could acknowledge that and at the same time preserve his proprietary feelings about her.

"This is Emmaline McClure," said Martha, "my dearest friend. You'll love this, Charley: she lives right on the other side of the kitchen wall, but she has to go all the way downstairs to get over here. The price one pays for privacy. We're thinking of having a door cut through. It's safe now. You'll love this, Charley: Harry had quite a thing about Emmaline, and I really didn't dare make it any easier."

The women laughed and Mrs. McClure gave Charley her hand. As his fingers scratched over a many-stoned ring, he thought that being set on honesty made a person inventive and exaggerating. He thought that Harry's "thing" about the woman was probably the size of a butler's pantry. Harry, alive, no doubt enjoyed every minute of it; dead, he probably would resent the hell out of it because it made him look just a little smaller than life-size.

Mrs. McClure sat back, releasing him to Eve, who was curled in her chair, holding her glass in both hands and gazing at him in a teasing, girlish way.

"For God's sake," he said, and he thought his voice was trembling a little, "grownup, married, and a real beauty. I wouldn't have known you."

"I would have known you," she said as he kissed her on the cheek. "You haven't changed at all. Except that the Texas sun has baked the hair right out of your head. All but that crazy little rim."

Charley touched his head and everyone laughed and he joined the laughter. Mrs. McClure tilted up her face and appraised him with brilliant little glances.

"Don't mind Eve," she said. "Isn't baldness supposed to be a secondary sex characteristic?"

"Women seldom are," said Charley. His voice was more impatient than just dry. He was impatient to get started with whatever it was he had come for, to share the grief or commemorate the dead. Something.

"Virility," announced Mrs. McClure. "Baldness is a sign of virility."

"Harry was as bald as an eagle by the time he was thirty-five," said Martha, "and so proud of it."

Mrs. McClure laughed and stood up and said she had to go and anyway no one had offered the poor man a chair. Martha walked with her down the hall. Two handsome women, Charley thought, with all their wits about them. The thought he then had he did not like, that Martha would no more now than ever pretend otherwise than the quid pro quo that had finally been devised between her and Harry. She was, in her own way, as honest as Helen was, just as Harry, probably, was a romantic like Charley, but saying Say it loud enough and it will be true, instead of Charley's Don't notice and it will go away.

Glancing about the room, with its long low emerald and sea-blue chairs and sofas, the kind of stuff that Harry would have thought shouted taste as loud as taste could shout itself, Charley pictured Harry striding the room, coming to rest by the marble fireplace. Bald as an eagle, beak like an eagle, claws tight around all the beautiful things, wings spread over all the beautiful people, possessive and proud, collecting his quid for his quo.

"I guess I gave you quite a shock," Spencer said, carefully insinuating into the silence his quiet soft Southern drawl. "I thought you knew about Harry or I'd have been, you know, slower."

Charley nodded. Spencer's face sent out a message of due solemnity and consideration and shrewdness. He wanted to like Spencer, to think that Eve was in good hands. Spencer was no eagle—bald or otherwise—and that was probably all to the good.

"I need a freshener," said Eve, abruptly, deliberately. "Who's with me? Mother let the servants off and no one will ask for a drink for fear of having to fix it. We're hopeless, Charley. We lead lives of loud indulgence."

Charley liked that and was about to answer when Spencer said, "I been working. I was right there at the old desk working away, wasn't I, Charley?"

"The old desk?" said Eve, rattling the ice in her glass and eying it with bored intention. "Not the new desk?"

Spencer laughed. "If you take out two glasses, mine's bourbon."

"I thought you preferred gin," said Eve. Her voice, though light and mocking, sounded dangerous. Looking at her, Charley saw Harry's bronze face ready to explode. Explode, he told the face; go on.

"Gin is perfume," said Spencer easily. "Evil-smelling perfume." The shrewd ingratiating face turned toward Charley. "Eve thinks Harry used to run me. She's right."

Without a word, Eve stood up and walked out of the room, and Charley quickly followed her. The dining room they walked through was a splendor, a Hepplewhite table on an off-white silk rug and silver and mirrors endlessly reflecting each other. In a stroke of forced relaxation, Charley hoped there was no manure or mud on his shoes to get him into trouble.

Once the kitchen door swung to behind them, he said, "Maybe it just makes it worse to talk about it, but I just wanted you to know how sorry I was about Harry. I mean, not just Harry but your father. In fact, not . . ." He started to say not Harry at all but because he was your father, but he realized that he was parroting Helen's sentiments and now, as then, they just weren't good enough.

"You were very close to him, weren't you?" said Eve. She got out an ice tray and handed it to him.

"Close?" Charley felt inadequate but he thought everybody felt inadequate in the face of death, and he felt phony and he thought almost everybody felt phony. "When we were kids, I used to think the sun rose when Harry did. Not that I don't now . . ."

"I never really knew him, as casebook as that sounds. Schools. Camps."

"Don't say that," said Charley, shaking his head.

She smiled. "It's true. I can't change it. But you two were very close, weren't you?"

Pulling the lever of the ice tray, Charley tried to think of a nice story to tell her that she would want to hear about her father. He remembered that when his own father had died he had felt deeply deprived of ever getting any true or full summation of him.

"When we were kids," he said, "we used to wear these knickers. You know, knickers, plus fours. Well, Harry had seen this picture of

Gene Sarazen right after a big tournament that he'd won. Sarazen's left knicker was falling down his leg. So from then on . . ."

"He was a pretty good golfer," said Eve, "but hardly a champion." She turned from reaching down two brown bottles from a high cabinet. The look on her face, a little wistful and fierce, as if she might come out with Goddamn, made Charley feel very close to her. "Do you think my father was a failure?"

Charley was puzzled and uncomfortable. Feeling stupid, he asked, tentatively, "Playing golf?"

"No, not playing golf," said Eve with impatience. "Me. Mother. This." Her hand swept the kitchen in a violent gesture, abruptly died on a brown bottle on the counter. "The fact that not one of us is really aching except you. If I'm aching, it's because I'm not aching. Never mind. Forget it. Poor Charley." With the last words, her expression shifted and he imagined that he saw ice freezing inside the crystal glass she held.

Charley said, "Thank you," and then, dropping a handful of ice back into the tray, "This is a nice kitchen." My brother has a very nice kitchen, he thought. My brother has a very nice daughter. Has? Had. Not his.

Back in the living room and seated with the others in a square around the square cocktail table, Charley said, "When's the funeral?"

"The service?" asked Martha.

Spencer said, "It was this morning at 10:00."

Abruptly, and in barely restrained fury, Charley stood up and walked to the marble fireplace. "What was the rush?" he asked. "I thought he just died yesterday." He knew, from their alerted eyes and mouths, that he was asking for trouble, but he thought that trouble was exactly what the death of Harry ought to demand of everyone because it was what Harry would have wanted. Well, if Harry, dead, couldn't bring it about, then Charley, alive, alive, could. For a moment he imagined that Harry was beside him at the fireplace, urging him on, allied with him against the others, all the others.

Quite sharply, Martha said, "It makes it worse to wait around.

The whole thing is barbaric."

"Harry hated funerals and stuff like that," offered Spencer.

"Not his own, Billy boy," said Charley, dismissing him with a wave of his hand. "He wouldn't hate his own funeral."

"What an odd thing to say," said Eve.

"You know what I mean," said Charley, whirling on her. "At least there was a time when you might have known. He would have wanted the whole show. He wouldn't have tried to kid himself with all this goddamn honesty."

Martha stared at him, seemed to be attempting to stare him down, seemed to settle for saying, "What on earth can that possibly mean?"

"I'll tell you what it means. It means he had a conception of himself. He would have wanted the mourners' bench and the widow's weeds and a big fat eulogy on Harry Williamson Osborn even if it was all Pure Crap. He would have wanted the whole world to think he counted big, even if it was a great fantasy. You and your being honest would have made him sick. It makes me sick. If you can't cry tears, you could at least hide your faces and cry the noise."

"You and Helen never had the same notions we had," said Martha, with simplicity and condescension and a measure of conciliation. "After all, you and Helen . . ."

"Oh, you needn't include Helen in it," said Charley. "She's honest, too; she didn't want to get gypped out of lunch. She hasn't lost anything. She never even wore knickers."

His harsh painful shouting laughter was mirrored on their smug and unbelieving faces. He knew that anger—his anger, loud and new and vulnerable—was worse than useless to beg what he wanted from them, a recognition of loss to match his sudden desperate own.

"You have no right," said Martha, cool, her wits still about her, but her expression now the sheath of the knife, "to come back here after ten years and sit in judgment."

"To sit in judgment?" repeated Charley, softly, struck by her words. "You're wrong. I'm the original avoider of judgment. I just came back to . . . not avoid Harry."

As if cut loose from a mooring weight, he felt adrift and very quiet.

He took his hat and planted it on the back of his head. He paused, decided to hell with an apology, and nodding to each of them he left.

When he walked out of the apartment building the air struck his face and made him squint. The doorman said it had turned colder and he would whistle up a cab. Charley said he would walk.

He crossed Fifth to the Park and went down a side path. He sat on the first bench he came to and lighted a cigarette by shielding the match inside his coat. He felt that he had the Park all to himself. Helen would be waiting for him to telephone, but he decided not to call her just yet, not, just yet, to face her truths, to compromise with her.

He glanced over his shoulder to the apartment house and counted up seven floors. There, leaning, supported by the marble fireplace, was the shadow of a man who was as bald as an eagle. The wind cut at Charley's eyes and they smarted and teared. And that was all right. Harry would have wanted somebody to cry for him, and none better to do it than his brother, who was aching, who had not known that, freed, he would need to ache quite so much.

End of a Game

Charles Andress once said, and believed, that he and his whole life could pretty well be summed up in eighteen or twenty categories, like sportswriter, husband, father of two, Democrat, ectomorph, WASP and so on. Of course he was not all that simple, but he believed himself to be usual, predictable, lacking in dark recesses. Therefore he was confused and shaken when he finally came to recognize that his wife's breakdown tyrannized over him, that he was unable to sustain even ten minutes without thinking about it.

If everything is all right between us as Caroline claims, he asked, then what could be wrong? With her? Me? His fingers pressed eight keys at once and jammed the typewriter. Answer the question: If everything is all right . . .

"Well now, how's our very own Grantland Red Smith Rice today?"

The face of Caroline, secret, sensual, smug (and sick, don't forget sick) vanished, and Charles looked up. Wilson. A lummox. Face like a pale tomato. A fair man, Charles chided himself that he did not have a quarrel with Wilson, who did not matter. With whom then? if everything is so goddamn all right?

"The boss says any time you say so, the presses can roll."

"I'm not finished," said Charles. He jerked from the typewriter the sheet of yellow paper on which, after a sixty- not a fifty-minute hour, he had written only the heading of his column. "If you think this stuff is so easy to write, try it yourself."

"What'd I do?" asked Wilson. "Pass along a message is all. I'm the boss? What'd I do?"

"You circle," said Charles. "You wait."

On a clean sheet of paper he typed his name and the name of his column: Now In This Corner. And relieved by that he remembered Wilson at whom he had thrown so small a punch. He said, "Sorry, I'm just edgy, I don't feel good. Look . . ." but he said no more and Wilson walked away, not mattering in the least.

As if he had been more badgered than in fact he felt he had been, Charles quickly fought back by writing: By rule this column has never taken sides in personal disputes between a ballplayer and a manager. But sometimes the soundest rule must be broken. This is such a time. The very public hassle between manager George Wain and pitcher Wag Schumpeter promises to wreck our small pennant hope. We must take sides.

Hooked. For taking sides was precisely what Dr. Loeb had done from the beginning. Hid it though. Sleek Loeb, extending a hand . . . of what? Charitable contempt? Pure deception?

"Naturally you are concerned about your wife," Loeb had said. "But of course you must realize that her difficulty comes from many years before your marriage. You are not responsible in that sense."

Charles had shrugged to convey that though he was no psychiatrist, he was no fool either, he understood something of breakdowns. Yet fool, he soon saw, was exactly what he was. It was days after the interview that he thought, My wife's trouble comes from many years before she married me and I am not responsible for it; the difficulty is not the result of our marriage, it is the cause; the difficulty led to our marriage; I am a symptom; I don't count.

If I am only a symptom, he imagined asking Loeb, how can she say everything is all right between us? Can everything be all right when I amount to so little? But if I were the cause, how then could anything be all right? And why, Dr. Loeb, do you who know her so little know her so well while I do not count?

Charles looked across the city room. A vast nervous amphitheater of a room, who could work there? The sports editor wore rimless glasses and weighed one hundred and twenty-six pounds and loved contact sports. Behind those rimless glasses, Charles thought, the harsh gaze was upon him: Can't do the work any more, Andress?

That morning in his unctuous sinister voice the sports editor had asked if Charles had anything interesting for the column. "For a change" hung unspoken between them. Grateful to have an answer at all, Charles said, Yeah, a good-old-days piece, about Wain saying Schumpeter ought to see a psychiatrist. The editor had said, Better leave that to the medics, don't get in over your head. Charles had said, I guess you think people are more interested in high school basketball? The editor's teeth showed back to his molars. Better make it good then.

Charles wrote, Things have come to a pretty pass when the manager of a contending ball club publicly suggests that the team's only twenty-game winner ought to see a head-shrinker. No, psychiatrist. Thirty years ago many a manager would have said that a guy like Wag Schumpeter ought to have his head examined. Today, it's Go see a psychiatrist. In the first instance, invective, pure and simple, the prerogative of men who nurse ballplayers. In the second, diagnosis, partial but nonetheless first-step diagnosis. The emphasis is altogether different. Now I ask you, if everything was all right between them, what could be wrong? That is, if Wain had properly managed the erratic southpaw.

He had been the one to get Caroline started with Loeb. Hundreds of details had finally culminated in one conclusive episode. The draperies of the house drawn all day, every day, yet not a lamp lighted unless he lighted it. Not one social engagement in months. And the fatigue, too fatigued to go out to dinner with him, to go to a movie or a game, to be with him. And all that silence too, which he, fool that he was, had chalked up to the natural leveling off of a marriage. Well, but she had never complained, never said a word, and the children were clean, fed, happy, miraculously undamaged. And of course there was his deeply held belief that theirs was a family graced by love. They quarreled so rarely, and when they did they were not killers, they split their differences. Oh yes oh yes, graced by love.

And then the one event he could not ignore or misunderstand. He had one day called home a dozen times, to get Caroline to go to the first night game of the season, and he had received no answer. He was not exactly worried, but by the day's end he was irritated that she had not anticipated that he might be worried. When he got home, eager to show off his annoyance, he found her sitting in darkness, while the children played in their rooms. He flipped the lightswitch, and he saw that her face was quite dirty, with driblets of food around her mouth, her hair was uncombed, and her dress was soiled and misbuttoned. She's off her rocker, he distinctly told himself, and the impact of the nasty phrase brought with it a strangling rush of terror.

Yet in his methodical, workmanlike, competent way, he set about rectifying things as best he could. After she went to bed, before 8:30 (and wasn't that a pattern he should have long since detected?), he called their family physician and got the name of a "very first-rate man," Rudolph Loeb. Next day he called and made an appointment for Caroline.

That night as Caroline headed for bed, he called her to him. He thought she had worsened even that day. She stood before him like a repentant child, head lowered, eyes averted, fingers twisting. First Charles attempted to enfold her with words of love and confidence. Don't charge in. He pointed out the tensions he knew she suffered, the problems, the boredom.

"You overload the system," he said, laughing hopefully, "and it breaks down, like an electrical circuit." He felt awkward and heavy of tongue, and he thought she ought at least try to help him; she wasn't a deaf-mute. Finally he blurted out, "I think you need a psychiatrist, I've made an appointment for you."

He anticipated wrath and defense. Indeed, her anger would in some fashion have given the lie to his fears about her. But she offered no resistance. "I know I'm sick," she said. "I've known for weeks I was getting worse. I thought you'd hate me for it."

As her quick tears washed grime and powder and yesterday's lipstick down her broken face, he rocked and patted her. He felt very tender toward her, and he thought he had handled the situation quite well. Momentarily he regretted going for outside help without giving himself a chance to help her. But that night he heard her weeping as she slept.

Caroline and Dr. Loeb set up a schedule. She would see him three mornings a week at 11:00. From the beginning, she had improved. Oh, not in a straight, steady line, of course, she pointed out, but more like the business of the spiral. Or maybe three steps forward and two back. At the end of the first week, and with visible effort, she opened the draperies on the side of the house that faced the woods, the private side. Still, going to the grocery store frightened her, and anyway she kept the street-side draperies closed.

For nine months Caroline visited Dr. Loeb three times weekly, one hundred and fifty minutes weekly, seventy-five dollars weekly (forget that, for Pete's sake) plus the cost of a baby-sitter (honestly!) and the operation of the automobile (who minds? who minds?) and how the hell long does it take the cat to climb out of the well at three forward and two back?

I have nothing against psychiatry, Charles wrote. In fact, I sometimes think that every lefthander worth his salt ought to have a few preventive sessions on the sofa. Lefthanders are notoriously unstable, they list the wrong way. I happen to be a fair sandlot southpaw myself, and no harm is meant.

"He's a dear," said Caroline one Sunday afternoon at the end of the first month of treatment. "A funny, old-world little man; you'd expect a thick accent, but he's been in this country since he was six. No accent, but all the rest. Maybe foreign men understand better . . ." She let the sentence trail off, and as if her love of sunlight had never faltered, she threw open the draperies on the street side.

"Don't I understand you?" Charles asked, idly.

"We're married, that's different," she said. She stared at him for a moment, looking stricken and afraid, and then she turned back to the draws of the draperies.

"Leave them alone," Charles said quickly. "I understand you with love, he understands you with his mind. That's the difference, all I do is love you."

"That's everything," she said, "as long as everything is all right between us, that's everything." And joyous, she came to sit on his lap.

"Damn the kids," he said, "Sundays were always the best."

She smiled with teasing pity, flirtatious and tender, a look he had forgotten that she owned, a look that stirred a desire that he had only been pretending to have. "Poor Charles, the kids are as hard on you as they sometimes are on me. Dr. Loeb said maybe we weren't quite ready for all the responsibilities."

"He did, did he. What else did he say?"

"Nothing," said Caroline, standing up, straightening her skirt. "He practically never says a word. Maybe he didn't even say that. Maybe I just thought he might. I do all the talking."

"And what do you say then? I mean, about me."

"Nothing. Just how much I love you."

"That's everything," he said.

That's nothing. Very suddenly, the fact of his immense ignorance erupted in him. He knew nothing about her therapy, nothing about her sickness, nothing about her. For this important time in her life, he was a stranger, a bystander. For all she apparently needed, she had Loeb. Bitterly he drew a poster: Andress Go Home.

He got up. "I think I'll pull weeds. Somebody has to do something around this place. And you know what else I think I'll do? Go have a talk with your boyfriend. If you don't mind, of course." Impulse had spoken, brilliantly. How marvelous and powerful he was. He grinned at her, a grin that felt like oil around his lips, with a touch of malice.

"No I don't mind," she said. "Dr. Loeb said he'd be glad to talk to you any time." His grin dried to paste.

For the next two weeks, Charles's fantasies broke with increasing insistence into his work and sleep. In the evening following her visits to Loeb, he spent restless, agitated hours attempting to pry out of her what had happened. He hoped he was subtler than he felt. I was thinking about your mother today, he said, meaning were you talking about your mother with Dr. Loeb? We ought really to talk more don't you think? he said, meaning Did you talk about me with Dr. Loeb? I don't feel so good tonight, he said, meaning Do you love me, do you tell the doctor that you love me? And it seemed that what

Caroline said in answer was always a kind of precise irrelevance. She told him, sometimes in detail, but she told him nothing he wanted to know.

Eventually he thought he detected a consciously devised pattern of telling intended to conceal, not reveal. Always she told him something outside herself, mother, friends, father. If he probed more deeply, she said Lord Lord I'll be months understanding that one. That evasion, too, he believed was calculated. But he was not sure.

Finally he decided that Loeb's willingness to talk to him should not keep a grown man from taking advantage of that willingness, and he went to see Loeb. He took his own lunch hour, and he thought he had taken Loeb's. I'll pay for it, he said. I'll pay the twenty-five an hour, just go on and take the rest of our savings. But the money was not at issue, and he denied to himself having thought about it. Other than just joking. A joke.

When he entered Loeb's office, he was unhappy and embarrassed, and he affected a nauseating jocularity not at all his style. Every aspect of his wife's condition was good for humor. When he told the doctor that he had recognized her illness because she was . . . dirty, he laughed. He laughed at his coming to see Loeb, lied and laughed that he was doing it to please the sick little girl (had even called her that). He finished up with a ribald psychiatric joke about the coarse sexual fantasies of a woman patient. He didn't think the joke was funny. Never had.

The sleek owl sat with hands lightly touching, the index fingers tapping on the bridge of his nose, rocking and twirling his large, blue serge buttocks in the pea-green swivel chair. The smile that was not a smile, not sympathy, but removed, distant, powerful understanding brought forth from Charles an abject question, a sudden pleading and surrender.

"What am I to do?"

The chair swiveled sideways and in that moment of silence Charles saw the bulging eyes, the beakish nose, the mobile, full lips. In a flash of rage, he asked himself why Caroline could not see all that vulgarity and egotism and sensuality. He came to his feet, his hand raised to forestall Loeb. "I'll just grin and bear it. Sorry I took your time." The decision was all his own.

"Just a moment, please," said Loeb. He motioned for Charles to sit. Sullen, nervous, Charles sat down, and instantly he believed that Loeb was about to tell him that Caroline was divorcing him. Why else had they wanted him to come? Why, if not to tell him this final irrevocably damaging thing, that Caroline did not love him? Why else had they connived to get him here?

"We never know," said Loeb, "why at any given moment a particular personality has what might be called a collapse, a breakdown. Sometimes there are more likely reasons than at other times. Naturally you are concerned about your wife, but of course you must realize that her difficulty comes from many years before your marriage. You are not responsible in that sense."

Shrugging, Charles gestured for Loeb to go on, he wasn't a fool, he understood the etiology. Momentarily he thought it would be fun to share with Caroline the asinine fantasy he had had that she was going to divorce him. But then he thought he would not share this with her when she would not share anything with him.

"Treatment," Loeb went on slowly, "is often very alarming and undermining for the whole family. In many cases it's a good idea for the wife or husband of the patient to have some supportive therapy. To help him through the trying months."

A key slipped in and turned a lock. Charles stood. "So that's it, so I'm the nut now."

Loeb was imperturbable. "Not at all. I only meant if the strain gets to be too much . . ."

"Look," said Charles, thumping his chest with his index finger, "I'm a measly sports-writer on a measly newspaper in a measly town. I have four mouths to feed and four bodies to clothe and four heads, at least at last count, to shelter. Bus fare is fifteen cents each way. Insurance, one hundred twenty a quarter. Retirement pension is twenty-five dollars a month, but what's twenty-five a month when it's twenty-five an hour. Savings? Going fast."

Loeb interrupted. "I'd be happy to arrange for the payments over a period of years. It is not uncommon . . ."

"It isn't the money, it isn't the money," Charles shouted. "If I woke up and found myself curled up like a baby sucking an inkwell, I still wouldn't indulge myself in these little chats with you. Maybe you ought to take up golf, that would kill a lot of time."

Dr. Loeb's face showed neither anger nor amusement nor even recognition. He said, "I didn't mean treatment with me. It's unwise for a therapist to have two patients from the same family."

Charles' taut spirit went flabby, but he gamely concluded, "Just don't you and Caroline get to planning anything for me. I'm a big boy, now. I don't think I could get sick if I wanted to."

Dr. Loeb stood in a posture of dismissal. "Of course it's purely up to you, Mr. Andress." And days later Charles thought, I am a fool, I don't count, but I am not sick.

Charles wrote, If Schumpeter put himself in the hands of a psychiatrist, then quite obviously control of the team would shift from Wain to the doctor, at least when Schumpeter was on the mound. The psychiatric relationship permeates all others. Put it this way: If George Wain husbands the team, the doctor is—no, for God's sake scratch that. Let no man put asunder the relationship between a ballplayer and his manager. Christ. Take the case, the real case, of James Piersall. Scratch out Christ, but keep Piersall. Charles reconstructed the case of James Piersall. It took two full paragraphs. That was nice. Facts, facts.

"I know you got more important things on your mind," said Wilson, "but these are times that try men's souls."

"What?" asked Charles.

"The boss says, 'See what's with Red Smith over there.' I see, I believe it's dolls. But Charles, friend, the out-of-town edition goes to bed in thirty minutes and you know it don't sleep good without that old Andress hot water bottle to snuggle up with."

"How do vultures know, Wilson, the precise moment to quit circling and go for the flesh? Smell? Sight? ESP?"

"How would I know?" said Wilson.

"The human counterpart," said Charles, "can spot a weakened condition ten desks off, knows a wound when it sticks its finger in one. You keep circling my desk and I'll begin to think I'm sick, dying, dead." I am sick, he thought.

"You sure talk sick," said Wilson. "Thirty minutes."

Charles said to himself, Thirty minutes. He wrote, All joking aside, it is not in the purview of the sportswriter to comment on psychiatry, pro or con. I am only pointing out the ramifications of Wain's contention. The real point is that when any manager goes outside the normal channels of communication between players and himself, he is only admitting that the battle is already lost. Time for a change?

He closed his eyes. Could he run it? Would they print it? Was it that much worse than yesterday's, that much better than tomorrow's? Would there come a time when he could not write at all? And so what? I'm dying, I'm going home.

He clipped together the two sheets of yellow paper, folded them lengthwise, wrote his name on the outside like a student, put on his hat, gave Wilson an ugly wink and floated out of the city room. Dolls, he thought. Oh to be Wilson, say to be racing home now for a quickie. Andress, ardent lover. Yet lover, he thought, was a role he played but rarely now, and with painful, unreleased, unsexual tension. It mattered too much now. Each occasion of their coming together he thought was an opportunity for a miracle, to reestablish them where he once had thought they were, graced by love. As each miracle failed, he felt farther from her, less her lover, profoundly desperate. And in a strange turnabout of their roles, it became Caroline who pursued him and with an apparent disregard for everything except pure sexual pleasure.

Ah darling (he pretended that he heard her say), we had such a good session today, Dr. Loeb and I, but don't ask what. Want me? Go to bed with me? Now now now. Thus the excitement engendered by Loeb found fulfillment with Charles. He was degraded. Even so, even so, he attempted to turn these seemingly unguarded moments into occasions for prying her secrets from her. With her wariness brought low by lust, what might he not elicit from her?

Answer: damn little. Even then, there she mastered him. He feared for himself: how long before the effort broke him?

Out of the aborted interview with Loeb had come his compulsion to trap Caroline into admissions she would not know she made. At the beginning, his little traps—suitable for snaring lies as well as truths, and for separating them—snapped shut often before he was fully aware that he was at that moment attempting to trap her. Innocently he asked a question; guiltily he listened. But eventually nothing was accidental; he knew exactly what he was about, was ashamed of it, and was exultant.

That first night after his visit to Loeb he had said, "Went to see your boyfriend today." He felt an acid anger, remembering the nasty phrase *supportive therapy*. "Maybe I will, maybe I won't."

"What?" she asked. "Maybe you'll what?"

In the mirror he watched his face, turned it right and left. "You know," he said. Conniver, name it. The first trap was thus set.

"No I don't," she said. "Tell me, tell me. He wants to send me away, doesn't he? Away some place."

Her mouth moved in the circular motion of her anxiety and her face grew haggard. Thwarted, stung, soft with love, he went to her.

"No, nothing about you. Me. He thought it might be a good idea if I get some supportive therapy. That's all." In the quiet moments before sleep that night he recalled Caroline's tears and he wondered if they were real or were the dishonest agents of the conspiracy with Loeb. He touched her shoulder and forgave himself.

Frequently in the following weeks when he thought he was at the point of an important revelation, she broke into tears. Her timing was superb. Please, Charles, please, what do you want, what are you after. The sad, broken, harrowed face. Always he was deeply ashamed and vowed never again to harass her. But even as he vowed, he saw forming on the edge of his awareness a new, more intricate plan. And when that too failed, brought on its accompaniment of tears, he roared with injury and anger, and planned anew.

Hearing the baby cry out in sleep one evening, Charles said, "I guess the kids really get their lumps in these sessions with Loeb. They sure can get on my nerves." He tensed, waiting.

She appeared thoughtful. "Well, today I told him we were getting Jenny a two-wheeler for her birthday. I guess I'm still uncertain about it. She's so little."

After a pause Charles asked, "What else did you say about her?"

"Nothing."

The trap snapped the air. Injured, he said, "Two-wheelers, the most important thing about your kid is a goddamn two-wheeler. For twenty-five an hour you sit talking about two-wheelers. You don't bother to say whether you love her or want to pinch her head off. You have a nervous breakdown, you say you have a breakdown, and your children don't count enough to even discuss them except two-wheelers."

She held out her hand. "Charles," she said.

"Or me either, I guess. What's the most important thing about me? That I'm a lousy sportswriter and you and your boyfriend are having a lot of sport on my twenty-five dollars?"

"Please don't," she said.

"Well what do you say then? What do you tell him that I'm too dumb to understand? What's he give you I don't? What are you trying to do to me?" When the echo of his anger died away, he heard her weeping.

"I love you," he said, searching out a talisman to quiet her. "Even when I think I'm losing my mind, I know I love you, Caroline."

"But you don't know that I love you," she said in a drowning voice.

"That too, mostly." He went to her and began to touch and pat her, tentatively as a small child touches and pats a baby.

In bed that night Caroline said, "You mustn't mind too much this getting angry."

"You just get well and I'll be all right."

"I think I am getting better," she said. "Of course it's a backward and forward thing. Dr. Loeb says . . ."

Dr. Loeb says. Charles sang out: Take me out to the ballgame, set me out in the crowd, buy me some peanuts and crackerjacks, I don't care if you never get well.

Like the traps, the explosions developed their own patterns, as if he were caught in a rhythmic cycle. Try as he did, and he did—smiling larger than he ever felt, talking desperately of other matters, even admitting his anguish to Caroline as if naming would relieve him—he could not control his outbursts. Nor could he confine them and his anxiety to his home. Shortly the quality of his work declined so that even he noticed. He turned in a shorter and shorter and duller and duller column later and later. His colleagues looked at him, puzzled. Look, he told the sports editor, my wife's not well, give me a break. This department rode me for three years, I was the only one anybody was reading and you know it. Can't I ride a while? The sports editor said, Buddy you been riding, what's the trouble, you splitting up with the wife? Hell no, said Charles, hell no, she's just sick. He walked hurriedly away, sickened.

For among the many visions that obsessed him was that of her having left him. Deeply grieved, he lived alone forever. Others found him tragic. Now that, he said to remind himself that he still had his good old sense of humor, is what I call funny. The scene shifted to comedy and Caroline and Loeb scampered off. The owl and the pussycat go to sea in a beautiful pea-green swivel chair. Floating amidst the high waves. Drowning. No. Danced by the light of the moon, the moon, they danced by the light of the moon.

Good thing he still had his sense of humor. Could still laugh at his wife. His sick wife. In the sudden inner quiet he heard the dying of laughter, and he longed to say, But what of me?

As he reached home, walking the block and a half from the bus stop, he heard the carillon of the Episcopal church sing out 12:00. As he put his hand on the doorknob, the significance of the hour came to him: Caroline would be bidding goodbye to Dr. Loeb, the small, soft fluttering hand held overlong in the moist, throbbing hand of the doctor.

"Hello," he called out when he opened the door. Silence. The house was empty. He thought he had never felt such emptiness before, as if it had been not simply departed but irrevocably deserted. In a rush of panic and passion, he went in a running walk from room to room, seeking out the signs of the final leave-taking. He found the kitchen as he had left it that morning, cream-sodden cheerios plastered on the sides of the bowl, a gnawed, damp piece of toast, a half-filled coffee cup, a nearly empty bottle of curdling milk on the drainboard. Caroline had left the mess to him. In her desperate desire to leave him, she had not had the consideration, that dreg of love, to clean up after their last meal together.

Methodically he set about straightening the kitchen, dropping the contents of plates into the disposal, rinsing, stacking, scraping fried egg off the formica table top, wiping indefinable nastiness from the high chair, and saying over and over to himself, This is really funny.

When he heard the front door open and close, he was not surprised. He knew he had been only challenging a toy disaster, only playing a game of tragedy. Whatever else was wrong, Caroline was not capable of an act at once cruel and calculated. He was very touched by this knowledge.

"Nap time," he heard her say. "You've had a lovely morning and it's time to rest, both of you now."

Charles lay flat against the wall. He did not want to see his children. He did not want to weigh them into whatever course he intended taking. What was it anyway? Why had he come?

When Caroline came out of the bedroom, he was standing in the hallway. She looked a question: Why are you here. Indeed. He shrugged: Just am. Mildly perplexed and expectant, she slipped her arm around him and they walked into the living room.

"Where's everybody been?" he asked.

"The sitter was sick." She explained that she had taken the children to a friend while she kept her appointment with Loeb.

"How was it?" he asked.

"Fine. They ate lunch and apparently had the time of their lives."

Charles gave her his rigid back to look at. "I meant Loeb."

"That was fine too. Why are you home so early?"

"And why are you evasive so early? And so late?"

Caroline looked puzzled. "Evasive?"

"Evasive," said Charles. "It won't work any more, Caroline. I want to know what's going on, I have that right. And I don't mean two-wheelers. I mean you. I mean me. Don't try to evade it. What did you talk about today with Loeb?"

"The grocery store," said Caroline evenly. "Why I still have to get there when the doors first open. Do you mind telling me what's going on?" She sat down.

Charles closed his eyes. Was he nauseated, or only imagining it? Was he dizzy? Sick? "Do you mind telling *me* what is going on? I'm home so early and so late for you to tell *me* what is going on."

"Tell you what?" she asked in a pinched voice. "Minute by minute? Word for word? 'Good morning, Dr. Loeb,' I said. 'Good morning, Mrs. Andress,' he said. 'Nice day,' I said. No, he said that. I said 'Yes isn't it.' "

"Laugh," he said.

"I'm not. But don't you see I just can't tell you bang like that? I don't even understand it myself yet. You're not a psychiatrist."

Charles sighed, for her benefit. For himself, he wept. "What did you say about me?"

"Your name didn't come up."

"I don't count," he said. "My name didn't come up. I don't matter." When Caroline started to stand, he shoved her back in the chair. The roughness of his gesture surprised him. He said, "Please, Caroline, help me. Don't you see?" With clenched fists, he was a supplicant.

She looked closely at him. "What is it you want?"

"What is it you want?" he mimicked her. "You don't even know there's anything wrong, do you? If I had both legs sawed off like bleeding stumps, you'd be more concerned with a pulled muscle in your little finger."

"I don't know what you're talking about," she said. She seemed puzzled, but oh so well, so reasonable.

"This: I have a wife and she prefers a stranger to her husband. I have a good job but I can't get the work done right any more. Don't you see what's happening? It's this simple: we have got to start thinking about me for a change."

He stopped, waited, expected her sudden tears. He feared them and he desired them. Waiting, momentarily he saw clearly that her crying gave him a kind of respite, meant she cared. Then cry.

"I think of you all the time," she said quietly. "I know this therapy is difficult for you . . ."

"Christ," said Charles. "You're not sick, you're not the sick one, I am."

"I love you," she said.

"Don't try that, I invented that trick myself. Love excuseth all things."

"I'm getting better," she said. "Please be patient. Please don't make it hard on me now."

He closed his eyes, felt the drumbeat of his eyeballs. "You don't care if I'm sick or well. I don't count." Action presented itself, a course of action sang clean, through all the noise. He opened his eyes and laughed close to her face, and he felt a tinny jingling excitement. He walked over to the telephone in the front hall and dialed the newspaper office.

Caroline came to stand beside him, her hand making tentative gestures of affection toward him. He ignored her. "What are you doing?" she finally asked. "At least tell me what you're doing."

"I'm quitting my job. I can't make it any more."

"Don't, Charles, please. This isn't good. Are you teasing?"

Teasing, did she dare ask teasing? "Wilson in Sports," he told the switchboard, thinking that it was fitting and proper to give the satisfaction to Wilson who also did not count at all. Heat rose in his face and filled his head and eyes and he felt tenderly sorry for himself. "You and Loeb, you and your boyfriend, you never gave a damn what you were doing to me. Well now you know."

Just before Caroline brought her hands to her eyes, he saw her face begin to sag and break. Never mind about that, he'd not fall for that again. She walked away. He looked beyond her to the living room. The sunshine was too bright, unpleasant, dust motes swam in the glare. But the pursuit of darkness was Caroline's way, not his. He would not close the curtains, he would choose another way. As he waited for Wilson, many books and stories, many case histories and even ancient family legends, pictures and fantasies of chaos and misery crossed his memory, and in each Charles Andress was the star. Yet none quite suited him, and so, waiting, he wondered on what downward spiral he would set himself—how, if not in her darkness or another's shriek, he would find his own escape. What awfulness awaited him? What safety?

But at once he faltered, for already he began to hear the sound of his wife's weeping, her shattered sobs. Not fair, not fair, he protested, this is my time. As Wilson said "Who is this?" Charles vowed he would not hang up the telephone, not surrender. But of course he did. All games must end for Charles. After all, he was who he was, and neither mockery nor longing changed that. Regretfully, he acknowledged that he was unable to desert himself or her.

She did not look up at the bang of the telephone. Her face was against her knees, her hands raised as if warding off blows.

"I'm sorry," he said. "I love you, Caroline."

Later, he thought, a small lie to his boss would tide him over, provide an excuse for his strange behavior. I thought I had something serious, he imagined himself saying, but it was only a bellyache. And tomorrow words would surely fall more easily upon the yellow paper, more quickly, better words, for surely today he had finally come against the limits of himself. And yet tomorrow night perhaps—he had to face this—he would again attempt to ensnare his wife in revelations; but his attempts would be half-hearted, useless, would not persuade even himself. And he would no doubt be furious again at his failure just as he had been today, but not so furious as today. He would again grow quiet as now he had, and sooner quiet than today. Eventually he might even forbear, since no other course was possible for him. He was, after all, a limited man. Limited. Momentarily he ached with that knowledge. And then he bestirred himself to go to his wife, for it was she who was sick, before whom opened darkness and flux, who needed him, toward whom he had a duty to perform. Whom he loved. Gently he stroked her cheek and allowed himself to ask silently, Well, she is sick, isn't she?

We Two—Again

Caroline taught linguistics at Boston University and had stopped off en route to a summer in Japan. Hartley lived in the hills behind Stanford where her husband was a professor of American literature. That's where they were, sitting in lounge chairs beneath a California live oak, two women, thirtyish, old friends from their Alabama childhoods. She's still pretty, thought Caroline. How handsome she's become, thought Hartley.

"You're still pretty," said Caroline.

"You've gotten even more handsome," said Hartley.

They exchanged admiring glances. They had once said they would spend their last ten widowed years together. Caroline had never married. They had not seen each other in five years.

"Tell me," said Hartley, sitting back, and Caroline did. Monographs written and others planned, promotions and even set-backs of a minor sort. Her shifting sensibilities. Wanderings. Adventures.

"Remember at the Alabama State Fair in the fall I think they called them Bumper cars? Dodgems? That's me. Bump and bounce off. That's the way I like it."

Hartley saw the tough little cars, heard the whirr of tires. Yes, Caroline was like that. Resilient. Even reckless. "Bounce off what?" she asked.

Caroline shrugged. "Still a lot of bumper cars out there. This morning on the plane from Boston . . ." But then she spied two little girls of ten or so peering around a bush. And so she did not go on with her story of the man against whom she had bumped, off whom she had so quickly bounced. Anyway, he lumbered, he twanged, he had not suited her. "Come out here," she called.

The two girls came forward, knocking together, clumsy as heifers, but something attractive about them, appealing. The little fair one had freckles. She hoped that was Hartley's.

"This is Adrienne," said Hartley, indicating the taller, darker of the two, "and this funny-looking chipmunk is Sara." She put her hand on the child's shoulder. "Mine, all mine."

"Not Daddy's too?" Sara said.

Hartley drew Sara into the circle of her arm. "What on earth's he got to do with it, for heavens sake?" She waited for a clever retort from Sara but Caroline, on the lounge shielding her eyes from the late sun, said, "So you're still the perennial virgin."

"So long," said Sara. "You aren't talking to us."

Hartley watched the two girls rush for the house. "Having a child," she proclaimed, "is like being in love with someone utterly self-centered and dumb and boring but you can't not be in love."

"You bear up awfully well," said Caroline.

"Now I feel better about it, if you approve." The sun coasted slowly behind the Monterey pines. This was the nicest time of day for Hartley: the slow drop into coolness after the heat, the bees swarming after the last of the sunlight, sometimes a hummingbird to visit her orange trees, and Richard soon to be home. Strange that she and Caroline had started so close and had ended so far apart. A whole continent.

Caroline glanced about her at the dark shingled house, the clumps of brittle shrubs, the strong gorgeous flowers, that shaggy tree just beyond the patio wall. Perhaps that was where the pungent smell came from. "It's really dry out here, isn't it?" she said. She rubbed her fingers and palms together. The sound was like stiff paper.

"I do spend rather a lot on Estee Lauder," said Hartley, "but I'd rather dry up and blow away than . . . molder."

"And of course I would rather molder," said Caroline. "But then you always were The Nice Girl."

It was exactly the right thing to have said. They laughed in acknowledgment and intimacy.

"Do stop that," said Hartley. "You make me sound so priggish."

"The Nice Girl," repeated Caroline. "How I envied you that."

She was pleased at the good feeling, the humor, that still flowed so easily between her and Hartley. She was glad she had decided, somewhat against her instinct, to stop over. Having rapport with Hartley made her think a little better of her youth. Perhaps it hadn't been as bleak and painful as she had thought. And sitting in the dying sun with a delicious coolness on her arms, she allowed herself the luxury of thinking of times back, that girl she had been. Waiting to grow up, to get out of that tight world where you had to be one kind of girl or you were out of it. Well, she had been another kind, perhaps an odd taste, but certainly distinctive. People had noticed, even then. Oh wouldn't it be loverly, the vocalist sang.

"Remember the high school dances?" she asked. "All those boys in their little black tuxedoes and us in pastel organdy."

"Yes," said Hartley. After a pause, she added, "I'm thinking of how you never would play their silly games. I admired that."

And then Caroline's memory cast up a sharper image of herself, the maverick, darkly glowering and miserable, rather hunched, as if to charge, desperately wanting, yet spreading unease around her like bad air from a cave. That was long ago, and so quite pleasantly she said, "You lie. You are thinking what a success you were and how I admired that. And anyway I never would what? I'd have anythinged, I'd have anythinged anybody."

Hartley laughed, as she was meant to do.

And there in Caroline's memory was Hartley laughing—fair, spare, light and happy Hartley—with damp gardenias at her wrist and a corps of little Southern gentlemen at her beck. And laughing now, still laughing as she gazed up at her own blue sky. Hartley's blue sky and Hartley's orange trees in Hartley's aged wine kegs in Hartley's garden and hummingbirds and ferns and straw and twigs enough to make the happy ending to it all.

If that was what you really wanted. Caroline turned on her hip to face Hartley and she said, "All in all I've been to bed with at least a hundred men beginning with do you remember that good-looking but slightly baby fat boy from the University of North Carolina the summer we were seventeen?" It struck her, too late, as an inordinate, even grotesque thing to have said.

Without so much as a pause, Hartley said, "The one with the little cluster of pimples at his mouth so he always seemed to be grinning?"

"Yes, that one," said Caroline. She subsided flat against the lounge chair. "The one with the pimples. I should have known baby fat wasn't punishment enough. I suppose Richard never had a pimple in his life."

"Nary," said Hartley. Slept with a hundred men, Hartley repeated to herself. That's appalling. And yet, quite suddenly, she felt lonely, remote, somehow diminished, as if pimples were a gift from that boy no one had ever offered her. Gift? Whatever, Caroline had been able to receive it, and she had not.

She heard herself say, "My life these days seems just the same. I don't do anything." And hated hearing that and quickly added, so quickly even she thought it was part of the same thought, the same intention, "Well, of course I wife. I wife. I mother, I. Miller, I. Magnin and I Saks."

Caroline laughed her easy low rich laugh and Hartley joined her. The flicker of an interval and Hartley began to ask, did Caroline remember this man, that old lady, this one and that, and Caroline said she had seen at the Met once in New York a comically obese woman in whose face she had at last unearthed the remnants of a friend from home.

Richard came home shortly after 6:00. The sound of his footsteps hushed their laughter and their remembering and brought their spirits up to the edge. As he walked down the lanai toward them, Hartley tried to see him through Caroline's eyes. His shoulders were perhaps narrow, sloped, but his brow was vast and elegant. Would Caroline think so?

Richard raised his arms in a large friendly greeting and shouted, "Caroline." He walked out to the patio and directly to her. Caroline shouted "Richard" and rose to meet him. In that moment, she saw him as he—as all of them—had once been, when Hartley had brought him home to be inspected, sporting his shiny new Vanderbilt master's—a year ahead of Caroline's—picked up on his way to Harvard. She had gone out with the two of them and a cousin of Richard's, a small-town lawyer about to be an alcoholic (I'm jes lunnin how to be a jerge is all, he said with every drink). She and Richard had competed and parried through the evening to a dead draw, while Hartley sat like a fairy princess and the cousin every once in a while whispered in Caroline's ear, Ma deah, you should lun to be mo' frivolous else you'll never marry. How trivial and dreadful it had all been.

She saw at once that Richard had improved with the years. His smile lifted the sides of his mouth, giving him a wolfish look that contrasted with his cerebral brow, a combination she quite liked. He kissed her exactly on the front of the lips, not sliding by in that false way she so disliked.

Richard held a paper sack in his hand and after he kissed Hartley he handed it to her and said, "I bought a lovely wine just to show our learned friend from the miserable East that we're quite civilized out here." He presented Caroline with a little bow and a nod, a parody of preciousness. There was still that boyish quality about him, his eagerness to please. These ex-good boys, she thought, make fine distance runners.

"Learned," she said, dismissing that.

"Miserable?" repeated Hartley. "That's sort of rude."

He threw up his hands, to show he had no chance, had never had a chance against such partners. "Educated?" he offered Caroline. "Muggy? Humid?" he asked Hartley. "Anyway, be careful with it. It's a '67 Bordeaux." He turned to Caroline. "I thought you were probably an expert. Of course Hartley would rather have cherry coke. You can get the girl out of the South . . ."

Hartley heard the grating of Caroline's laughter. Of course she could have laughed too, had she chosen. She chose not. Somewhere inside her something chose not. She said, "You sophisticates, professors, bon vivants." Though she turned up her lips to show she too could joke, she felt the rise of her resentment, a foolish unworthy resentment. Couldn't he be allowed to tease her? He often did. And of course he too would be a little uneasy, with Caroline there, would need to tease. But he shouldn't have done it in front of Caroline, whom they had not seen in so long, who had had no experience in the teasing play that went on between people who had been together for years.

She spent the next twenty minutes in the kitchen, inefficient and alone. Her husband. Her friend. Gliding down the lanai to fetch Sara, she cast little smiles out to the patio where ice tinkled and gin-and-tonics fizzed and the talk slid back and forth as the light fell. In the kitchen water boiled. Out on the street, children screamed.

After half a hamburger, Sara said, "I don't want any more," and, raging, Hartley swung from the range where butter sizzled and spat, and in a voice she herself heard as menacing said, "Eat."

The child lowered her gaze to the table. Was this threatening beast the nurturing contented mother? Hartley swiftly drew up a chair beside the child and with her arms spread gestured the child to her. They held each other a moment. She felt the warmth of the child's body, the softness of the skin. A fragile thing, in her keeping. She said, "Would you like Adrienne to spend the night?" Sara gave her a kiss and went running out of the house, down the drive, calling her friend's name.

Richard heard the child and smiled. Caroline liked the privacy of that smile. He was, she decided, appealing in an old-fashioned, Anglo-Saxon way. If she said that aloud, he would see the humor of it. They would laugh together. The evening air was surprisingly moist. It was not a bad place, no vibration of heavy trucks, no angry bleating of horns, no endless hum of machinery. Good smells, too. That odd odor.

"Smells like Vicks Vapo-rub," she said.

"Eucalyptus," he answered. He pointed to the tree beyond the wall. "Eucalyptus. Nice sound, isn't it. It's Greek, I suppose. Covered. Covering."

"Yes, Greek," she said. They sat in silence for a moment, and she listened to the rattle of the leaves of the eucalyptus. She thought that Richard was watching her, and she instinctively tightened her elbows at her sides and that lifted her breasts a little. She did not turn to face him, to break the spell of his watching, but she imagined the alert shy eyes, the assured mouth.

Hartley stood in the doorway, an outline, a lonely pale figure, Caroline thought, against the expanse of gray light. Faded out just a little, a little tighter, a little more sparing even. That was too bad.

Hartley said, "Dinner, you two."

Once Caroline was seated, Richard uncorked the bottle and Hartley, at the sideboard, put slices of rare beef masked with bearnaise sauce on warmed plates. Broccoli with butter. Crisp potatoes Anna. Earth colors on earth colored plates. Handsome. I'm an artist, she said to herself.

Richard said, "That looks really good," but she did not respond.

As he ate, he told an intricate anecdote of a faculty meeting in his department in which petty empires crumbled and the New prevailed. He was oh so charming, oh so attentive, Hartley thought, his eyes shuttling between them as if carrying messages. I have no messages. At the end of his story, he said, "The less at stake, the more vicious the politics."

Caroline gave her rasping laugh and Hartley forbore to point out that she had heard that before.

Through that course, through the clearing of the glasses, deep into the salad, Caroline and Richard talked. They talked of tenure and budgets and the taming of students, and of their work. They were, Hartley thought, like two men. The thought gave little satisfaction. Two men would have paid her court, jumped up when she made her entrances, made her the bull's eye they aimed at. But Caroline was the bull's eye, Richard was the bull's eye. And she was merely the jealous onlooker, and that was so absurd.

She rose, repentant, but she found herself saying, "I've baked a marvelous crusty cherry pie with love and duty," though in fact she had made a blancmange.

The refrain swept through Caroline's memory. "But I can something something hide?" she asked. A poet she and Hartley had read aloud to each other. Millay? Wylie? "Whose is it?" she asked, fanning the air to rouse up the past.

Richard said, "Sounds like one of Hartley's lady poets." Hartley disappeared through the swinging door to the kitchen. Richard scratched his ear and looked troubled.

Caroline said, "Yes, she used to be able to quote gallons of it."

She still could not remember whose poem it was. With love and duty but I can something. So long ago. She had indeed shared so much with Hartley. They were in their teens, it was late at night, and they read poems aloud to each other, each pervaded by inchoate longing. Odd how vulnerable some memories made one feel, how the past seemed as sharp as the present and made a brand new wound. The women poets from the twenties or was it the thirties and how she and Hartley had imitated their spit curls and worn that blackish red lipstick when everyone else was fading into pink. "I don't suppose anyone reads them any more," she said. She wondered if Hartley did. "You know, they were like cats, curled in on themselves, licking themselves."

"Licking their wounds," said Richard in a distracted way. "Will you excuse me a moment."

He went into the kitchen where Hartley was lifting blancmange onto chilled crystal bowls. "Good," he said. "I'd much rather have that than a cherry pie. Can I help you?"

"You cannot," she said and he said, "Can you please tell me what crime I am being punished for?"

"Did I say you had committed a crime?"

"You look, you act like I have. She's your friend."

"Ah," she said, and this helping of dessert plopped onto the bowl and broke in half, "if you had a friend we could have a foursome."

He sighed twice (she heard regret, disgust) and returned to the dining room. He had not said the magic words, whatever they were. She knew she was unfair and she wanted to say, It's not you, it's me. And then perhaps he could say the magic words that would set her right. When she brought the bowls to the table, she heard, from Richard, "As it turned out, it was strictly a blind alley."

"What alley have you been skulking in now?" she asked. She had meant it to sound amusing, to be a way of giving in.

But it was a bit late. "Poe. Chivers. Who stole from whom," Richard barely managed to get out.

Caroline said, "I honestly never heard of what did you say his name was?"

"You had to be from South Carolina. Thomas Holley Chivers was his name."

Sara and her friend stood in the doorway in flimsy nightgowns. Sara said, "You got to be kidding, nobody's name is Thomas Hardly Shivers." The two girls bawled out their laughter and fell limp in each other's arms. Richard threw back his head and joined them with a volley of hard proud notes.

At a signal from her father, Sara came to the table. He gathered her onto his lap and they rubbed noses and foreheads. He looked over the child's head at Caroline and Caroline narrowed her eyes in response.

When Sara started to leave, Caroline said, "I'm very pleased to have met you," and held out her hand.

"Kiss Caroline, Sara," said Hartley. "Go on, kiss Caroline. She's my best friend from the old days, you know. Go on." Her voice was rough, insistent. The child hesitated, then slowly turned to Caroline.

Caroline thought the child was going to refuse. She felt the rise and focus of anxiety, the heartbeat in a sudden freefall through her chest. As the child approached, Caroline tentatively, ambiguously offered her cheek. The child leaned toward her but her lips did not touch. Had they noticed? It was Hartley's fault, as always. Hartley had always managed somehow to make her feel bleak, sterile, unlovely.

Hartley was pleased at Sara's coldness. "Was that a kiss?" she said. "Come here, little love, and get a kiss."

At the door Adrienne said, "I'm tired and I want to go to bed right now."

Hartley said, "You come get one too."

"I don't want one, thank you," said Adrienne.

"I don't either," said Sara. As the two girls walked away, Hartley made a show of pretending to be pretending to be hurt. Richard shook his head in sympathy.

"How sharper than a serpent's tongue it is to have a thankless child," he said.

"Tooth," corrected Caroline.

"A serpent's tooth," said Hartley. "Even I know that."

The women exchanged falsely complacent looks. Richard smiled, a cold show of tooth and lip. Caroline found him distasteful, like stale water. She preferred a richer mix. She did not like his pale brow or his prissy eyes. She glanced at her watch and feigned surprise at what she saw there.

"I told a friend I would meet him for a nightcap at 10:30," she said. "The sound of the silver horn," she added to Hartley. Now that was Wylie, she was sure of it.

Hartley saw the darkness of streets where strangers met. Dark glowing men she would never know. Adventures she had never had, would never have. Free to do as she wished, to say yes and no. She would never know all that, she would never be strong enough. But Caroline was, had always been.

"The sound of the silver horn," Caroline repeated. Yes, that was the very essence. Open, alive, unbound. And yet lately with the throb of Brahms or Mahler swelling through her apartment, she sometimes felt quite alone, too much alone. Suppose she died and went unnoticed for days, with only the whirr of the turntable to break the silence.

Hartley longed to go back to Sara's room, to close the window against the insidious bay fog. Perhaps she would claim from the sleeping, slightly opened, warm lips the kiss that had been denied her. She looked at Richard. Later tonight they would talk of Caroline. Of her verve, her openness, her losses. She reached over and touched Richard's hand.

Caroline dropped her napkin alongside her plate and stood up. She would go back to the Fairmont for the nightcap she had halfway promised. She thought of the rather stocky man with the bushy blond mustache and the Midwestern accent who had sat beside her on the plane from Boston. She knew he would be there, waiting. She could when she wished have someone waiting for her. She felt weary, the long day, the time change, but she would meet him. Her visit of duty was concluded. Actually the man had been rather attractive, one of those men who keep their eyes right on you to see every nuance of your response. And if he didn't please her, she would simply turn away. In any case, tomorrow she would be off to Japan.

Richard turned a final splash of wine into each glass and the three saluted each other. They smiled wonderfully open, friendly smiles. They raised their glasses and the light of the candles glinted in the crystal and in their eyes. To old dear friends. To old good times.

One of These Days . . .

They closed the windows every night against a hoped-for rain, and by the time Ralph Pickens got to his office in the morning the air was stale and hot with the June sun. They wouldn't also lower the shades. Twice Pickens had left notes taped to the shade, saying If you pull down the windows, which you needn't since it won't rain until July 4th, pull down the shade or leave the oven door open one or the other.

Twice he had found the notes untouched, the windows closed, the shades up. Each time he thought, So okay I'm only assistant solicitor prosecuting crimes the newspapers don't even know have been committed and even the niggers can ignore me. That was the way they got back at you, through you at everybody. He had vowed never to leave another note until he was sure it would make them look smart and do what he said. And they would some day, when he was chief, and nobody would push him any more.

"If I were chief," Pickens said, "I'd invest a little money in the life span of my assistant. Do you know how much a cooling unit costs, Charles?" He dropped his briefcase on the desk and swung around to bang up the window.

Charles Winthrop said, "It is right warm in here."

"About two hundred dollars," said Pickens. "If the old man had thought in April to spend two hundred dollars making life bearable we'd have a clean docket by now, instead of being a month behind. I'd have finished this Brasher business with you instead of waiting for it to finish me. Go on, sit down. What's on your mind?"

"Well," said Winthrop, "I just wanted to talk to you another minute about Miss Brasher."

Winthrop placed himself on the cracked-leather visitor's chair and folded his hands between his knees. In his middle thirties, his skin was as dried and cracked as the chair he sat in, an old man's skin. But except for that, Pickens thought, his face was like a young girl's, taking everything for granted, inviting ridicule and trouble. Pickens had had to stand up for him many times because of that face and the feelings it revealed. Charles assumed everybody started where he started and ended where he ended, but the truth was his principles were other people's jokes.

"You're a fool, Charles," said Pickens. "You're about the best fool I know, but a fool all the same. You get out there in front of that jury and Miss Brasher that nigger and you'll get her the electric chair instead of just the five years I aim to make them give her."

"Let the miss go then," said Winthrop, smiling his soft smile. "But can't we settle this thing without taking it to the jury? She's just a kid."

"No nigger over thirteen is just a kid. I swear, the day hasn't hardly begun and I feel like my clothes been pasted on me with glue. I already decided to prosecute it straight through, no holds barred, even if it is against you. Anyway, there isn't anything else happening in the courthouse today and we got to see the newspaper boys earn their keep." He couldn't help smiling. Maybe for a change somebody besides the judge and the bailiff and the jury would know about one of his cases.

"You'd look mighty big," said Winthrop,"asking probation after you got in court. For a colored girl. That'd make a nice headline." He said it with an effort to appear off-hand, as if he didn't mean to be pressing Pickens's vanity. Nothing worse, thought Pickens, than a man trying to use tricks he doesn't even understand. But he knew then that Winthrop must be dead set on the case, dead set to do something.

"You see too many movies," he said. "The voters want convictions, not heroes."

"Before the trial then," said Winthrop quickly. "Ask the judge for probation before court opens. She's just a kid."

"Five years," said Pickens. Fending off Winthrop irritated him. He didn't like to have to justify himself, or defend his actions. "Even under the law she isn't a kid, she's nineteen years old and all I'm interested in is the law, not any of your psychological tests or nothing. I'm paid to make sure the state gets justice under the law is all I'm paid for. That girl was grown enough to shoot a man, she's grown enough to pay for it. I swear, sometimes I wish I was skinny like you. I reckon you don't even feel the heat."

"I feel it some," said Winthrop. "If she was your sister, wouldn't you have shot him for her?"

Pickens laughed out loud at that. Nobody but Charles would ask a white man to put himself as brother to a colored girl. "If she was my sister I wouldn't be what I am to make the decision. Most like I wouldn't have shot him because I'd have been in jail already for shooting somebody else. You can't change their spots, Charles. They are what they are."

"Now wait," said Winthrop as he leaned forward to catch Pickens's gaze. "The law is supposed to be color-blind. You can't judge like that, just because she's colored. And especially you. You have to know why she shot him, you have to know the circumstances."

"The jury'll do that."

"The jury'll do what you tell them." Winthrop said it as a fact, but it showed respect too and Pickens couldn't help smiling.

"Well, maybe," he said, "but this ain't open season on every man black or white suduces a girl." He plucked his shirt off his chest and fanned himself with it. "Let's talk about something besides niggers, Charles. You're crowding me. I don't see you often enough these days to spend the time quarreling. How's Sarah?"

Pickens wiped a handkerchief across his carefully bland and inexpressive face. He was sure his face never told a thing he didn't intend it to tell. It didn't tell how irritated he felt most of the time these days or how irritated he was with his friend.

He had been assistant solicitor for four years, handling the nasty little cases while the chief took the juicy ones with headlines, because they involved white people. The chief opposed the big lawyers, matched wits with real wits, and when he went down he went down in a blaze of community-wide indignation. Damn the jury, the people said, the papers showed the man was guilty, he should have got the chair. Even when the chief lost, he won.

Not Pickens. Even when he won, which he did most of the time, he lost because the cases he tried were sordid, involved colored people and nobody cared. Who cared that Jewel Brasher shot her boy friend? Throw her in jail and forget it. Only Charles Winthrop, who took the case for the promise of ten dollars he didn't even expect to collect and who acted as if it were Queen Elizabeth on trial for shooting Nasser. Well, Winthrop could afford to fool around because he wasn't going anywhere. But Pickens was and he hated every case he tried.

One of these days, he told his wife late at night, I'm going to get out of all this. I'm going to get in something has some dignity. The old man is never going to die, he said, he's seventy and he's good for another twenty years. I'm not waiting around until then, I'm better than that. Do you want a pheno? his wife asked. I can whip up a jury better than any man in this town, he said. I think I might run for Congress, I might just run for sheriff. Goddammit, he said, those black bastards have about killed my chances in this town. I'm associated with them in the public's eye. Do you want a pheno? his wife asked. They'd just as soon kill each other as not and I got to spend my life putting them in jail so the state can feed and clothe them for a couple of years so they are healthy enough when they come out to kill somebody else. Goddammit. Do you want a pheno? his wife asked. Goddammit, he said. Goddammit yourself, his wife said, you can't sleep so you're going to make sure I can't either, is that it? Goddammit, said Pickens. Then he turned over to go to sleep, thinking One of these days . . .

And now here was Charles Winthrop, his friend, but a man who never had a case worth twenty-five dollars that wasn't given him by the court and paid for by the state. A good fellow, but a jack-leg lawyer. Here he was, still wearing his winter tweed suit and still wearing that unconcentrated look of taking everything for granted and still thinking platitudes were worth ruining yourself over. And worse still, trying to make Pickens think so too. Here was Winthrop, looking at him as if he, Pickens, had committed a crime instead of just preparing to prosecute one, asking for too much mercy and not enough justice for a girl who wasn't a murderer for the simple reason that she couldn't aim that straight, but who had tried to be with as much malice aforethought as she was capable of. Asking Pickens to damage his career for the likes of her, as Winthrop had so often damaged his own until there wasn't any more damage to do.

"Now, Charles," he said, not waiting for Winthrop to say his wife was fine, "I'm not a hard man and you know it. I've done as much as anybody you can name to see the niggers got a fair shake around here. Didn't I get the grand jury to no-bill that kid that gang of fellows brought in here? Why, somebody else might've got that kid a couple years assault for fighting back against those fellows."

"That was fine," said Winthrop. "You were right."

"But I can't let my feelings . . . I can't let your feelings interfere with my duty. What would the chief say if I settled this one with you at the last minute when we got it locked up? Friendship, he'd say. Dereliction of duty for the sake of friendship. He'd have my scalp. I'd be the laughingstock."

"And you'd never be chief."

"Goddammit," said Pickens, "put it like that if you want to. There're worse things than wanting to be chief. What the hell do you want from me?"

Winthrop laughed softly. "Justice," he said, making a large deprecating gesture, "and a little mercy. If you don't object to the terms. That girl had cause."

"Who doesn't? Who ever shot anybody without some kind of cause?"

Winthrop stirred in his chair and gazed at his thumbnail. "Have I ever asked a favor of you, Ralph? Any kind of favor?"

Now it was coming, Pickens thought. The touch of the friend, the demands of old acquaintance. Grow up with somebody, go to law school with somebody, share office space and they're in you for life for just one little favor, waiting for the opportunity to ask one little favor. High principles or not, a man who had hold of a handle tried to use it.

"No, you haven't," he said. "You never asked me a favor and I just hope you don't. Not in something like my duty. And I'm right surprised at you even thinking of it. You."

Winthrop smiled, or rather smiled deeper because he always seemed to smile soft. "You don't understand. I'm not asking any favor for myself."

"And don't ask any for her either."

"Well, all right, or her either. I know you pretty well, Ralph, you have to admit that. Well, as well as anybody can. We've been friends a long time and it's a friendship I value. I've always cared what happened to you, inside and out."

"Same here," said Pickens, looking down at his desk. A friendship he valued. He knew he meant it. Little soft high-minded Winthrop. "You know that. What about that favor?"

"Now don't get mad at me," said Winthrop, holding up his hand. "Take it like it's meant. There was a time I wouldn't have thought to say this, Ralph. But I don't know."

"Say what?" asked Pickens, looking sharp at Winthrop.

"Before you get that jury in a lynching mood, forget you're the assistant prosecutor wanting to be chief. Forget all that. Just think about what that girl—black or white—did and why she did it, think what it meant to her and think what you yourself feel ought to be done to her. You yourself. That's all."

Pickens smiled at Winthrop, and turned away to smile some more. He glanced at his watch and dried his brow again. Old Charles. Pulling out all the stops to plead for a nigger girl. One of his lost causes. Sweating out the platitudes. You had to admire Charles, and you had to pity him too. A failure, but a decent good failure. Only, who ever noticed how decent and good? Who noticed who didn't resent it or laugh at it?

"You can ask that kind of favor any time and I won't mind, Charles. I reckon occasionally I do need to be reminded of my double duty, and I'm glad to have you be the one to remind me. I wouldn't take it from many and you know it. But the trouble with you," he went on, not angry but wanting a little something in return, "is, you never saw a guilty person. They say the prosecutor, the prosecutor's mentality I reckon they call it, never can recognize an innocent man. But the fact is not many innocent men get hauled in by the cops. And that's a fact. And it's my duty—not just my pride like you think—to prosecute them."

"But this girl . . ."

"Guilty," said Pickens with finality. "First of possessing a gun without a license she snitched off her sister's boy friend. Second, of concealing that gun on her person and toting it 15 miles in a public conveyance. Third, of shooting an innocent man through the shoulder in broad open daylight on a busy street with the risk of killing any bystander happened to be there. An airtight case."

"Innocent man?" asked Winthrop.

"Now, Charles," said Pickens, feeling weary, "I don't like that nigger any better than you do. Most like less since I've gotten a real bellyful of his kind being in this office all these years. A real nigger Don Juan, full of lip and sass. But he's not on trial. He's just the girl's victim and my star witness." Quit nagging, he thought, I've had enough.

"It's just too bad she aimed so high, for the sake of a few other colored women."

"You got so you like that little nigger gal," said Pickens, laughing, as he walked toward the door. "You like that little gal, don't you, Charles?"

"Well," said Winthrop, following him, "I reckon I do. Aren't we supposed to protect the innocent and don't we like what we protect?"

"Okay, okay, you made your point real good," said Pickens, thinking Why can't he touch earth just once, why can't he like her because she's a hot little number, instead of liking all those worn-out words?

As the two of them walked down the cool stone corridor of the courthouse, Pickens began to tense with excitement. Yessir, he thought, an airtight case. And the only one on the docket that morning, so the newspaper boys would be in and out, earning their keep. And the courthouse regulars would be dozing on the back rows. And who could tell what might develop? Who knew when the assistant might catch fire, really burn up the jury, show just how good he was? "It's going to be hot as hell in that courtroom," he said.

He had hardly taken his seat when they brought the woman in. Dark as the bark of a tree, thin and long-legged, moon-faced with her full mouth kept tensely closed, only her lips, not her teeth, touching. The dress she wore, bright green rayon silk with pockets and neck covered with fragments of dull glass beads, was limp and too large and yet too short. Not exactly prepossessing. Why hadn't Winthrop told her how to dress, to come plain in a cotton? Still, she looked more absurd than dangerous, more kitten than cat, and Pickens allowed himself a moment to be glad of that for Winthrop's sake.

Catching the eye of one of the jurors, a fat-faced heavy-featured laughy type in a bright sports shirt, Pickens grinned and shook his head, to say, What else can you expect from *that*? The juror laughed back and nodded agreement. One down and eleven others would be easy.

Pickens could size up a jury in no time, scratch the mavericks to get just the right balance of harmony and discord, so they thought they'd earned their pay yet came quickly to a decision. The chief had to admit that no one else was as good at selecting juries, not even himself. Often Pickens was called in on the big cases to help with the jury, then sent back to try the nasty little ones that didn't even get mentioned on the eighty-fifth page of the Friday paper. And you could bet nobody gave him credit when the chief won, though the jury was the biggest part.

But this time he thought it might be different. He had thought that before but he thought that this time he thought it in a different way. There would be a few on-lookers this time. Are already, he thought, looking to the back of the courtroom where a dozen old men and two old women were taking seats. Maybe even one of the clubs, the Junior League or something, would send in their women to see how justice was meted out. He was sorry it was Winthrop, but still he thought, Look out, Charles, I'm right hungry.

The first three witnesses, all Negroes, told the same story, told it as Pickens had told them to tell it, building slowly, surely, with a touch of drama and a touch of humor, shaking their heads in wonderment, rolling their eyes as the climax approached.

That gal was holding that gun straight out like with both hands, and that fellow bellowed once and then he fall like a big old oak tree. Plump. Like that. That little gal never tried to get away or nothing.

Don't tell us what you think, Pickens said, just tell us what you know for a fact. I know for a fact she never moved, boss, they said, indignant. He had no call to criticize and make them look foolish like that. Pickens winked at the jury. Feisty, that's what they were.

And each time Pickens bowed to Winthrop and offered the witness.

Yet what could Winthrop—diffident,courteous, vague—do? Ask a few routine questions, which he did, act as if the whole episode saddened him in a highly personal way, which he did, and then ask, knowing it didn't matter but hoping the clue to acquittal might miraculously appear, "How would you describe the expression on her face when the police came?"

Why, no way particular, they said. Just standing there with them two children hanging on her, one on her leg and one on her arm. How, asked Winthrop, could she hold a gun in both hands and at the same time carry a child in her arm? She was carrying that baby, they said, sort of slung over her shoulder, like a coat she didn't want to put on. You know.

Pickens turned to the jury. The fat laughy man frowned in wonder and disgust. Shooting a man while an infant was slung over her shoulder. Winthrop didn't know what helped his case and what didn't. Dumb to emphasize that. It would disgust anybody.

The victim was Pickens's last witness. Knife-slim, neat and gaudy. On his way to the witness box he stared constantly at the judge, bright-eyed, promising to give a good, a splendid account of himself. Not exactly prepossessing, but that hardly mattered. One look at him—the suit too bright a blue, the yellow suede shoes, the long stiff hair curling over his collar, the fingernails polished into little mirrors reflecting light—and the jury knew what he was. But the important thing was what she was, and the jury would know that too, when Pickens got finished.

The man told his story with relish and, Pickens thought, intelligence, adding nothing, not too packed with detail, yet complete. So the fellow says There's a gal outside looking for you. I figure it was some gal, I didn't figure it was her with them two kids. But the minute I seen her I says Hello Jewel honey. Like that. Hello Jewel honey. Real nice. I didn't see no gun until it was shot, and the blood was just squirting over my coat. Sport jacket. I reckon I did bellow. That gal is dangerous. I mean dangerous. You know what I mean? Dangerous.

"Objection," said Winthrop automatically. Not even he seemed to think it mattered. The jurors smiled at Pickens and sighed, and they all seemed to be saying, Airtight, what a waste of time on a scorcher of a day like this. Still, Pickens thought, finish the building, add the roof, close the door. Admit every point the opposition might be planning.

"All right now," he said, "so the good men of the jury will know the truth of this matter, tell them what your relations with the defendant were prior to the shooting. And remember, you're under oath. Perjury is a serious offense in this state." Good little touch, that one, one he often used on witnesses the jury might find distasteful. Show them you at least are up to nothing.

The man grinned slyly, proudly, foolishly, and glanced at the judge as if the judgment rested there. "Well, you see now," he said, "I reckon I took her out to ride a couple of times. And you know . . . You want I should say?" Pickens shook his head. "But so did ten twenty other fellows."

"You say ten or twenty other men," said Pickens. "Can you give us their names in case we need to call them? These men who . . . took her out. You're still under oath."

"Yessir. James Webster for one. That how come I met her. One evening he is coming to town and bringing two girls and would I enjoy meeting them. I like meeting people I don't know already and

I said that'd be fine and one of them was Jewel."

"Anyone else?" asked Pickens.

"I seen her at the skating rink lots and I seen her at the show some and I seen her hanging round a place on Fourth Avenue and she's always hanging on some man. And I seen her . . ." Pickens cut in.

"We get the picture. It's too hot to prolong this trial any longer than needs be. These gentlemen would like to get home out of the heat quick as they can. Your witness."

As he sat down Pickens glanced around the courtroom. Two newspapermen had taken seats on the front row. Bored, disgruntled, irritated, they sat in identical postures, their heads thrown back with their necks resting on the top of the bench and their feet thrust crossed in front of them. On the back rows about thirty spectators dozed or stared vacantly out the window. Damn, Pickens thought, I can't help it if there's nothing here.

Winthrop rose slowly from his chair beside the girl. "I suppose it isn't too hot to get at the truth," he said. "Are you the father of this girl's child?"

As he spoke there was a slight stir in the courtroom. Even the newspapermen lifted an eyelid to stare at the defendant. Maybe something juicy, maybe not. Jewel Brasher sat as if she hadn't heard a word, her hands quiet in her lap, her face blank. That was the way they were, Pickens thought, they don't care about anything, dignity or right or anything.

"Well now," said the witness, looking sly, "ain't who is the father of a child what they call hearsay evidence?"

A shout of laughter broke from the jury box and the newspapermen grinned with closed eyes at the new twist to the old joke. Pickens felt a flush of pleasure. Maybe yet, with that to put in it, the story might see print.

"You have no idea," pursued Winthrop, humorless and patient, "if this woman's child is yours?"

"I don't rightly know how you'd tell," said the man. "That little child don't favor me any more than lots of others do. I can't claim 'em all." The courtroom laughed again and Winthrop turned to the judge.

"Your honor," he said.

"The witness must answer the questions as they are put to him," said the judge.

"I be frank," the man said, grinning with pride, "I be honest. I ain't denying nothing under no oath. It could be my kid, it could be ten twenty other fellows! Girl like that, it don't much matter who aims the best. Ain't nothing to be proud of if you accurate there."

The jurors laughed again, leaned forward to laugh some more, to be ready to laugh. Pickens laughed with them. Good witness.

"Your honor . . ." began Winthrop. But he stopped and lowered his head. He was gray with anger and he was humiliated. Poor Charles, Pickens thought, making bad matters worse, turning a lost cause into a farce, letting a sassy colored boy use him as a butt and suffering, as Pickens knew he was, not only for himself but for the girl he was holding up to the ridicule of her victim. I'm sorry it's Charles, Pickens thought, but I can't help it. He ought not take just any case.

"If the state is finished," said Winthrop in a muted voice. Pickens gestured to his witness to leave the box and the man walked long-legged and grinning past the jurors. Jewel Brasher, Winthrop's only witness, was called.

As she answered the token rote questions Winthrop put to her, her voice was soft, mushy, abashed. She stared with concentration at Winthrop, intent on pleasing him. Pickens knew the type. Shy as hell with whites and a real back alley she-devil with blacks, a menace to every man who accepted her invitation. Five years, he thought, might be enough to cancel that invitation. Didn't Charles see it? That she not only was going to be locked up but that she ought to be?

Gently, monotonously, Winthrop carried her over the worn ground of that day, coaxing the answers out of her, admitting every detail. Finally he asked, "Why did you shoot him, Jewel?"

"I told you, Mr. Winthrop." She stared at him with wonder.

"I remember, Jewel, I remember every word you told me. But I want you to tell these gentlemen too. I want them to know it."

The jurors leaned forward, hoping for something new they could laugh over, and when she said, "He's my baby's daddy but he didn't marry me," they leaned back with boredom and became aware again of the hot sun beating on their heads from the windows behind them.

Winthrop glanced around, perplexed by the change of mood in the room. Pickens had to smile. Old Charles had as much sense about a jury as a first-year law student. He'd never learn either, never comprehend the human factor. He took for granted the world cared as he cared. And he would always be wrong.

"Are you sure, Jewel?" Winthrop asked. "He says anyone of . . . of several might be the father. What about that?"

"Oath or not, he lied," she said. Nothing more, as if her saying it made it so. Pickens imagined that she had told Winthrop that weeks before, and she expected everyone to believe as he had.

Winthrop sighed. For a moment he seemed to be preparing another question. Visibly he shook his head, sighed again and said, "The defense rests." And before their eyes, the eyes of the jurors, the spectators, the newspapermen, the defense did not so much rest as it simply gave up. Not even Winthrop had hope left. Yet as he walked back to the table, Pickens knew, he was blaming himself, not the girl. Every dinky case he had he thought had victory in it, if only he were more competent.

It was Pickens's turn with the girl and as he strode toward her he felt mildly ashamed to take such advantage, felt ashamed as people sometimes feel they ought to feel ashamed. But he wasn't after Charles; he just happened to be in the way. Out of the corner of his eye he noticed that one or two of the jurors were already beginning to smile, aware as he was of the hilarious point to the whole hilarious business. Charles should never have tried to justify such a feeble case. Plead for mercy. Plead how the kids need her. Plead she's learned a lesson. Don't claim she had the right.

"Jewel Brasher," he said, making an obvious effort to remove the smile from his face, "have you any other children besides the one you claim this man fathered?" He watched the jury, wanting to be sure they were alert to his close reasoning.

"Yessir, I got Ben."

"And how old is Ben?"

"He be three next time."

"Well, now, Jewel," he said, "have you ever had a slip of paper attesting to the fact that before a qualified representative of the state you were ever wedded to any man?"

"Sir?" she asked.

"You ever been married, Jewel?"

"No sir," she said. The jurors laughed a little, wanting to laugh more, and the girl looked at them with a half-smile.

"I appreciate your forthright answer," said Pickens. "Now. Is this man whom you admit you shot last April the father of your first child? Did he father Ben as well as your baby?"

Oh he was going good now, rolling along, pulling the jury in his wake. And he knew, without bothering to look, that the newspaper boys and the spectators were listening too and he knew that he'd get an account in the papers at last. And seeing it, the chief would say, Well, Ralph, I hear you did a job. Want to try something a little bigger? Meaning, Don't push me, boy, I'm moving on. Oh yes, Charles had provided a wonderful new angle and he was going to do it fine.

"No sir," the girl said. "Ben's daddy was somebody else."

Pickens stepped back, mock surprise on his face. "I'm not keen today," he said. "You say you shot this man because he fathered a child by you. But you have another child by another father. Is that right?"

"Your honor, I object," said Winthrop, rising in his chair, looking now more angry than humiliated. He looked at Pickens and shook his head in angry wonder. "This isn't a vaudeville show."

"Sustained," said the judge, hiding his smile behind his hand. "Just ask your questions, Mr. Solicitor, and let the pyrotechnics wait until the summary."

Pickens nodded to the judge, and, nodding, laughed to the jurors. Then he leaned toward Jewel Brasher and spoke in his hardest voice, his fast, hard, overbearing voice.

"Did you shoot him too? Did you put a bullet through the head of Ben's daddy? And these ten or twenty others, if they had been less fortunate or shall we say more accurate, would you have shot them? Are you going to try to kill every father of every child you have? Will there be a colored man left in this country when you get finished?"

With that he let his triumph go, gave one loud shout to start the laughter, looked intently from juror to juror to make sure they got the point, looked at the newspapermen to see them writing it down. He led the laughter that swelled the courtroom, the jurors first, the newspapermen, the bailiff, the judge, finally the spectators awakening and joining fully. It was Pickens's finest moment. In four years of waiting and hoping, he had never so completely taken command, showed, goddammit, just how good he was.

And just as quickly his laughter, though not the uncontrollable crowd laughter of the courtroom, died away as the girl's voice got to him.

"Nobody but him ever promised to marry me," she said. "Nobody but him ever promised to give the boy and me a home."

"What?" asked Winthrop, who had come to stand between the girl and Pickens. "Say that again."

"He showed me the home where we'd live," she said. "I waited but he never come again. It was light gray."

Winthrop grasped Pickens's elbow and gave him a turning shove. "Tell them that and make them really laugh," he said.

"You're out of order, Winthrop," said Pickens. "Sit down."

"Well at least you see it," said Winthrop. "At least there's enough left in you to see it. Maybe not to do anything about it, but to see it at least."

Pickens looked down at Winthrop, at his excited tired old face. All right, he thought, I see it. Promise and trust. Maybe she did know what dignity was.

"You're out of order, Winthrop," he repeated. "We'll have to talk about it later."

"Later? Later? When it's too late?" asked Winthrop. "You still going to ask for five years?"

"Why ask me," said Pickens. "I just work here."

"You have the first say. They'd listen if you explained it." Winthrop's voice was barely audible in the excitement of the courtroom, the loud laughter pushed further for enjoyment not of the joke but simply of laughter. "It's what I was trying to tell you. I wasn't lawyer enough to bring it out so they could see. You were."

"Don't be a fool, Charles," said Pickens. "Ruin it for them just for a nigger gal?"

"Yes," said Winthrop. "Ruin it for yourself just for a nigger gal. Ralph."

Pickens stepped back.

"You think you're so goddarn high-minded, don't you, Winthrop?" He turned and walked away.

It took the jury ten minutes to find her guilty and she was sentenced to five years at Mary Willoughby Prison, and the bailiff (he laughed whenever he could catch somebody's eye) took her arm and led her out, with Winthrop following. And that night Pickens saw it in the newspaper on page two. "And the solicitor, Mr. Pickens, asked the defendant . . ."

"Well," his wife said, wrapping her arms around his neck while she read the newspaper account over his shoulder, "I reckon you're right proud of yourself."

"I reckon," said Pickens.

"I reckon now you'll bide your time and not be thinking of running for sheriff or anything."

"That's right," he said.

"I reckon Charles Winthrop knows who's the best solicitor this county ever had. Everybody knows it now."

"Leave me alone, goddammit," he said, pulling away. "It's too hot to have somebody crawling all over you."

"Well I'll be," said his wife.

Martin Fincher, Tripod Man

"Count on me, Mr. Hughes," I said. "I'll be there snapping pictures. Only, do I have to go by jet? They won't clean up the mess before tomorrow, will they? Anyway, I thought I was the New York expert; how come you're sending me to Mississippi?"

"Case wants you," Hughes said. "He asked especially for you."

"Fifty thousand feet is a pretty long fall, even to work for Case," I said. "And basically, I'm just a tripod man."

Hughes said, "Are you kidding, Fincher?"

"Sure I'm kidding," I said, and I was and I wasn't.

"All right, then," he said, locking it up. "Case will meet you at Idlewild."

I thought, that little son-of-a-bitch isn't going to hold my hand all the way to Memphis, watching me make a fool of myself. I walked toward the door and I said, "Case is the greatest journalist in America today; it'll be a real honor taking the pictures he tells me to." It was a dumb thing to say. I knew I wouldn't get away with it.

Hughes said, "What's the matter with you, Fincher? You don't want to go to Mississippi?"

"What's in Mississippi? Ain't it hot enough here?"

Hughes gave me a long, dull look. "A tornado," he said, "twenty-eight corpses, a wrecked town. Isn't that enough?"

Oh Jesus, you not only have to do what they tell you, you have to listen to that crap. "It'll be a story," I said. "Sell a hundred thousand copies at least."

I was pushing Hughes pretty hard and he didn't like my tone any better than I did. The difference was, he could stop it and I couldn't. He said, "A lot of photographers would like a job on this magazine."

That is the way they work you. You get all the connections plugged up on one side and they sneak around and plug in some other place. And with me, there is practically no way to avoid getting in. They don't even have to try hard and they've got me jumping.

"Not any photographers as good as I am," I said, and walked out.

That was 11:00 in the morning and I had until 2:30 to worry about it, worry about being the nastiest little coward in the world. A big lummox like me. Afraid of a jet airplane. Afraid of what I'd do once I got on one. Afraid I'd be the typical fool I am.

They say the thing to do is, don't think about it. Think about something else. And I tried. I thought about beautiful women in honey mink, looking like the Twenties. They had mysterious, shadowy smiles and their faces were half-covered by hats made of a dark silky stuff. And an egret, tickling me in the face. Egret. Bird. Birds flying. And I was right back where I started, worrying about myself.

When I was a kid I heard a traveling preacher talking about how adultery in the heart was as bad as in the bed. It seemed to me that was asking too much, judging too hard, and I made up my mind I was an Old Testament type, deeds not thoughts. I gave up controlling my thoughts, but I can at least try not to act them out; I can at least behave like everybody else.

I took a taxi home and I pretended I didn't mind the elevator ride to the sixth floor, but I did. When I went in the apartment, my wife was sitting with her feet up on the ottoman reading the *Partisan Review*. Dirty ashtrays and last night's drink glasses were still on the table.

She said, "What're you doing home, honey?"

"Same thing you are," I said. "Nothing, not a damn thing."

"All right, Martin," she said, putting down the magazine. "What's wrong?"

"Wrong?" I said. "Maybe you haven't noticed what a mess this apartment is." I was getting ready to let her have it but she started laughing. Nobody laughs like Elizabeth. She laughs right at you, asking you to join in and laugh at yourself. The funny thing is, it doesn't hurt a bit when you do. So I relaxed and laughed too.

She said, "When you get home at 5:30, the place is neat. If you had wanted a hausfrau you should have married a hausfrau. Did you want a hausfrau?"

The truth is I had wanted somebody who laughed like Elizabeth. I said, "Always my dream girl read the *Partisan Review* all day long. I've got to fly down to Memphis with Jonathan Case this afternoon, to take pictures of the tornado in Mississippi."

"Jonathan Case," she said. "Must be important."

That irritated me and I said, "Crap. Can't you just see his column on it? While the Congress frolicked on the lawns of Capitol Hill, a town of average Americans found itself face to face with nature's indifference to human aspiration."

"He's a little pompous," said Elizabeth, "but he always comes through with the right idea."

"Pompous?" I said. "He isn't pompous, he's flatulent."

She laughed a little and she said, "I'll bet it's even hotter in Mississippi, but at least you'll be air-conditioned on the way down."

On the way down. I said, "For Christ's sake, can't you think of anything but the heat?"

"What is it, Martin?" she asked.

I had been her husband for ten years and she didn't know. Why should she? I'm a genius when it comes to hiding. I never told her, never let her see. Afraid she'd hate me for being afraid. All my life it's been that way. Once I jumped off a cliff into a dime-size lake for a girl whose face I can no longer recall. And I parachuted at a county fair for a lousy roommate I toured the country with. Oh yes, deeds not thoughts.

But when nobody is looking, I give in. I hire a man to fix the rainspouts on the summer place, to put new shingles on the roof. Am I a workman? I should dirty my hands? And I scoff a lot. Tenzing and Hillary give me a pain. Skiing is for kids. When brave men are swinging on the high wire, I'm buying popcorn. I can't even watch them when I don't have to. I know I'm a coward, but no one else knows.

So I said to Elizabeth, "Nothing's wrong, what would be wrong? I just came home to get my stuff."

"Is it the airplane?" she asked. "You're afraid of flying, aren't you?"

I almost bawled, right there in front of her. Elizabeth. Elizabeth. Touching deep. And all the cursing and the wisecracks and the anger I'd invented vanished, and there was just the fantasy of fear.

The clouds are beautiful, I tell myself, thick and pink and soft, and if my camera was loaded I'd have a fine picture. And that's all there is to it. The man in front of me snaps his briefcase closed and it is a dull sound, and then it is an explosion. The airplane splinters open and there is a rush of choking wind and I am falling in space.

The man with the briefcase turns around and says to me, Got a match? I tell him no and we both look down and I'm holding a pack of matches in my hand. But what good are they? They are wet with the sweat of my palms. And the man sees and he laughs and I'm a fool.

"Crap," I said, "flying is safer than an automobile."

I went over to her and bent down and began to nibble at her lips. I knew what I was doing, I've done it too much not to know. And I knew it was useless too. Drown myself in love and awake sweating with fear. But so what.

"I'll be gone twenty-four hours," I said. "That's a long time."

Elizabeth whipped out of my arms and smiled, jollying me. "What a deprivation," she said. "Twenty-four whole hours."

"Come here," I said.

"Baby," she said, "it's just too hot and I'm just not interested. You don't want me if I'm not interested, do you?"

Yes. I wanted to say. To hell with you this time. In love you go out of yourself; in fear you go in. And I wanted out.

"All right then, goddammit," I said. And I picked up my things and left there fast, before I would say, You'll be sorry. Behind me I could hear her calling, "Martin, Martin, what is it? Tell me what it is?"

So I went out to Idlewild an hour early and got a ham sandwich and a Coca-Cola and watched the planes take off. And if I wanted one to crash I didn't know it. What I thought I was doing was going in the cold water toe by toe, so Jonathan Case wouldn't see the goose-flesh.

I hate Case. I hate him for a very simple reason: he made me look like a bum to myself. He's wizened and scrawny and prissy-looking and his face is covered with liver spots and he has a high empty voice. But he has courage, you can depend on him. He landed at Omaha Beach with the first wave. And he was at Inchon too. Once, after the pilot was shot, he had piloted a helicopter and landed it on a flattop in the middle of the Formosa Strait. When they got the door opened, he wasn't sweating, he wasn't even grinning—just saying, Help this man; he's hurt.

I was at Inchon too, and I was up in a helicopter too, taking aerial pictures of the invasion. That's a recollection that ought to satisfy any man, but I can't stop it there. The pilot said he would hold her steady and I could open the door and get a picture right on top of them. Just the thought of it was sickening but of course I did it. The wind was beating in my face and I saw two landing craft explode, smack together and explode. It looked as if someone had dropped a box of wooden matches, bodies flying all over the place. The camera slipped from my hands and went out the door and sank in the surf. And that time the thoughts and the deeds got mixed up and I reached back and grabbed the pilot by his shoulder and I said, "I almost fell, I almost fell, you son-of-a-bitch."

"But you didn't," he said, pulling loose.

Later that night I was lying on my bunk pretending to be asleep and Jonathan Case gave me a poke in the back and said, "Rough luck, Fincher, all that derring-do for nothing."

I said, "If the magazine didn't have you, it wouldn't have anything, would it, Case?" He shrugged and walked off and I knew he knew.

When we got back stateside, Hughes called me in, looking sour behind his oak desk. I thought, I've had it, all the way to Korea for a pair of wet drawers and all the way back to get sacked.

"Jonathan Case had some mighty fine stories," he said. "We had hoped to run a special, if we'd had pictures."

"I won a prize last year myself," I said. "Remember? Family of the kid strangled the old man in the park. Even his baby sister looked like an ancient black Christian."

"I remember," said Hughes. "It was taken in the living room with the crucifix hanging on the wall."

"Civilization takes place in the living room," I said.

"Case said the place was crawling with newspapermen," Hughes said. "Case said he really had to use influence to get you on that helicopter. Case said . . ."

"Case said, Case said," I said. "Just what did Case say? I suppose he thinks a picture is no good if I don't get killed taking it."

"Just the opposite," said Hughes, looking mild and puzzled. "He says you're a photographer, not an acrobat. He says it's a waste of your talent to put you on that kind of job."

I said, "I don't need Mr. Case's patronage but you tell him I appreciate his trying." And just saying it I felt like a bigger fool than ever.

"Well," said Hughes, "I think he's probably right: you're too good for the routine action pictures."

From then on, the action jobs went to the other photographers and I got the character stuff, portraits of generals, murderers, lovers in Central Park on the first day of spring, the kind of picture you look at for pleasure rather than fear or horror. I resented it some, but I was glad because I was good at it, the best, and it didn't scare me.

Case and I hadn't seen much of each other since Korea. He got too important, making pronouncements on the ways of the world. But I guess he still thought of himself as a reporter and I guess he saw something in the tornado he could build into a homily. And he had asked that I go with him, to get the human interest pictures. Martin Fincher, tripod man, flying down to Memphis, and afraid to fly.

Who has choice in this world? I do what's expected like the next man. I go to cocktail parties and I drink too much on New Year's Eve; I put a twentieth of my salary in common stocks and I see the new musicals. And when they tell me to fly to Memphis with Jonathan Case, I protest but I do that too.

I was the last passenger to board the flight because I didn't want to sit next to Case. Pretty little girls greeted me at the door, polished smiles and glassy stares. Better somebody homely and hot. Looking over their shoulders I saw Case in a window seat and I saw that he had put the Occupied sign in the aisle seat next to his. Three rows up I saw an old lady sitting alone, kolinsky furs and white gloves and a navy blue hat, and a vacant seat beside her. Can't I even sit where I goddamn want? I asked myself.

Why ask. I sat down next to Case, holding my camera gear on my knees, and I shook his hand. Case is courteous: he took hold of the handle of my camera bag, about to shove it under the seat. But I held on, I wanted something to hold on to. He laughed.

"Afraid somebody will steal it?" he asked.

I said, "This bag is worth over a thousand dollars. If we have an accident and I get out I'd just as soon not have to come back for it."

He gave me a prissy look. "That's one good thing about airplanes," he said. "No such thing as a little accident. I think I would prefer to be killed outright than seriously maimed. How about you?"

I decided to stay clear of that precipice. "Same with me," I said. "I wouldn't want to be maimed."

But as long as he mentioned it, I had to think about it if I didn't have to talk about it, and I had to admit it just wasn't so. Let Martin Fincher vanish finger by finger, hand by hand, not all at once. Better yet, I thought, take me out of here witless and toothless when I can't even tell you my name. Don't let me know I'm dying, even for one mad instant.

That's been my trouble all along. Everything that scares me leads to dying. The first time was when I was five, lying under the gables late at night. How does a kid come to think about death? Who knows. I was sitting high in a high tree on a platform I never built and a large gray eagle swept down and grabbed me by the neck and carried me thousands of feet into the dark sky. And the eagle let loose and I came floating slowly toward the earth and I knew that I would die.

I feel soft when I think of that little boy. I see him in white flannel pajamas decorated with little blue violins and horns. He never closes his mouth all the way, full of wonder and adenoids. I feel kind toward him, kinder by far than toward the man he became. Lima, Ohio. What a scene for the existential moment.

I went out of that bed fast and flew across the floor and out the door yelling Mother, Mother. Downstairs playing chess with my father. They are good old folks now, reading and rereading letters from their scattered flock, framing every picture of mine printed until their walls look like an obsession with the famous of our time. Their being still alive is a kind of talisman for me and I hate for the telephone to ring late at night.

They didn't hear me and I didn't go downstairs. One of those absurd incongruities that have plagued me all my life. I was afraid I'd get my tail switched or that my father would laugh. Next day I asked what was out in the sky and what happened when you die. My mother said I should have called her the night before and she told me about heaven. But I didn't believe her because she didn't believe herself. You just keep falling until you are nothing. So if you ever catch me singing Yankee Doodle or Alexander's Ragtime Band, it's because I don't want to think about what I'm thinking about.

The door of the plane clanged closed and I was imprisoned. The plane began to move. I gave out a sigh, a shudder, and quickly turned it into a bored stretch and slipped down lower on my backbone. I didn't want to see the plane leave the ground. I closed my eyes and rubbed them, attracting the sensation there, away from the nausea, the heat of my face, the sinking of my belly.

"Got something in your eye?" Case asked in that high voice of his.

I laughed. "A hangover," I said. "Didn't know I was flying down to Memphis today. Must have been 3:30 before I got in last night."

It was a lie, but I thought I'd make up a big story sufficient to cover any sins I might commit on the flight. But just then the plane arced to the right and I saw the ground out of the opposite window and the trees falling backward like dominoes and I couldn't help saying, "I haven't been in an airplane since we got back from Korea."

"I can understand that," said Case. "You had a pretty rough experience out there."

"What do you mean?" I asked, and I thought I might just give him a crack on his jaw.

He said, "I remember your pilot had you pretty low when those landing craft exploded. You might have developed a thing about airplanes."

"Oh that wasn't anything," I said. "It's just my wife won't fly, and so I haven't had any occasion. Just thinking about it makes her sick. Last time . . ."

But I stopped. I felt sick at myself, and cheap, and I thought: Elizabeth, forgive me. But she wouldn't have cared. She was brave and so it didn't matter to her to be called a coward.

"Go on," said Case, folding his hands. "Fear is the most fascinating emotion a human being has, the most various and individual. In sex and anger we're more alike, but in fear we're different."

"You don't say?" I said.

"Yes," he said. "The trouble with the psychological studies of fear is that none of the psychologists has ever seen it except from behind a desk in a more or less social situation. And one man's story is about the same in the telling as another's."

"But you have seen it," I said, "in the raw."

"Yes, I have," he said, "perhaps more than my share. I've been considering doing a paper on my observations."

I looked at him straight and I thought, Did it ever occur to you that you are the most flatulent man since William Jennings Bryan, that you aren't afraid because you're too busy worrying about your wind? And thinking that, I felt some better and I said, "Ought to be interesting."

"I hope so," he said. "Tell me about your wife; tell me your observations!"

"Look," I said. "She's just doesn't happen to like to fly. Anything wrong with that?"

"It's not unusual," he said; "who does?"

And there I was again, out in the middle of nowhere. We didn't speak for a moment and I felt the engines vibrate through me and I wondered when the inevitable would happen, when I would make a real fool of myself. I leaned back in my seat and pretended to fall asleep in my living room. Like the airlines claim, just like sitting in your own living room. Crap, I thought; I've never been in a living room twenty-five thousand feet above ground and still climbing.

Before I said it I knew I was going to, because one of the most certain things in my life is that if there is anybody within shouting distance I make pretty sure he knows what an ass I am about airplanes.

"Hey, Case," I said, "do you smell gasoline?"

I thought, This time I'm right, it really is leaking gasoline. The odor was strong enough to be almost visible, floating around us. Of course, I think that every time, but I thought I thought it this time with a difference, that I was right this time.

Case sniffed a little, looking sour and unfriendly. Then that old dry mouth of his cracked open, making his face look almost like a skeleton, and he laughed. "This is a jet," he said. "I doubt you would smell gasoline."

I laughed too, I gave it all I had. Let the fool recognize himself and thus cease to be a fool. I laughed hard. "Must have been that ethyl I drank last night," I said. And then, half to get it said and over with, and half because at that moment I felt it, I said, "Seems to me we're losing altitude." Quietly I said it, so sly perhaps he wouldn't hear me. But Case is no man to toy with.

"Are you sure you don't have a thing about airplanes?" he asked. His face was concentrated, thinking about me, analyzing me, understanding me.

I said, "I do not have a thing, the thing, anything about airplanes. What I do have is a dislike for people who talk in café society clichés and think they are being highly perceptive."

He gave me a small-eyed look, angry and belligerent, and that gave me some relief, a subtle satisfaction of my spirit as if we were finally even.

He said, "Fincher, this may pass for tough-guy humor . . ."

But the loud-speaker started to squawk and cut through his voice. "Ladies and gentlemen, this is your stewardess. We have had a fire warning in one of the engines and we are returning to Idlewild. It will take us approximately five minutes. Please fasten your selt belts and refrain from smoking."

"That's a damn fool thing to say," said Case.

"What is?" I said.

"Fire in the engine, we're going back to Idlewild," he said. "This ought to be interesting; some damn fool is liable to panic."

I said, "It'll give you a chapter in your book. If you make it."

The stewardess walked down the aisle, casting looks like rewards for fastened seat belts. She came to me and I thought she paused and I thought she gave me a pretty long look. It crossed my mind that those nice little girls had been trained to detect the signs of panic on a face. My face. I gave her a cheery smile, but I didn't want her to leave me; I wanted her close. A real pretty girl. I thought if she stayed close perhaps I'd do all right, I'd perform all right for her.

When she turned away I reached out and she looked back and I saw her face good for the first time. Heart-shaped face with a fringe of hysteria. I knew that she couldn't help me, she couldn't watch me, she was too busy watching herself. And I knew it was serious this time, it wasn't just me being scared. And I gave in.

My seat was wrung loose with the explosion, torn loose, spinning in space and I was in it, and I was falling and I was going to die. Around me floated the other passengers, kolinsky furs whirling and white gloves waving in the shattered wreckage of the plane. In the seat floating next to mine was Jonathan Case, liver spots and all, watching me with a notebook on his knee. But for the moment I didn't care because when you're dying how can you care? You can't lift your knees and you can't turn over and the air is close and heavy and damp from the earth. Only you don't even know that because you don't know anything; there is not even that to know. You can't even care that you're dead. There is only nothing. I thought, What is nothing? And I called out and no one heard me.

Case said, "Are you all right, Fincher?" His voice was full of concern and there was concern in his face, and I thought that was one more way of leaving me behind. He had the power and the right to feel sorry for me.

"Sure," I said. "How about yourself?"

He smiled faintly and nodded, and I thought, He's scared too. Jonathan Case is scared, by God. Or was he? Or wasn't he? But it didn't matter. The thing that mattered was that, scared or not, he was acting like a man. I thought, This time I'm a man too and I'm going to behave like a man. I can't help what I feel, but by God I am going to behave decently like a man for once in my life, standing on my own two feet.

You tell yourself something like that and it's fine and dandy, but doing it is another thing. I thought, If I had something to do to relieve the tension I'd feel better. So I opened my camera bag and took out the Speed Graphic and began trying to get inside to clean it a little. But I couldn't work the catches. My fingers looked like slabs of wet potatoes, and I thought, They're not me, don't blame me for them. I put the camera back in the bag and it took all I had to sit there quietly, with my hands resting on the bag and my face like a mask. But I thought, If I get Charley horses in both arms and both legs I'm not going to move. And I didn't.

"We're coming down now," said Case in a flat voice.

I looked out his window. Why do a damn fool thing like that? The nose of the plane was down and we were over a patch of water and I thought that pilot was mighty careful to avoid the residential areas. We straightened up a little and the landing field was right in front of us. Five thousand people were packed along the fence, and the red fire trucks and the red-and-white ambulances raced down the field. I thought, Now I'll have about ten seconds to think about it.

There wasn't a sound in that airplane, except for the passengers moving their clothes over the seats, as if they were collecting their things. I looked around the plane and there wasn't an expression on a single face. They were looking out at the scenery on a Sunday ride in the country.

I looked at Case and he was looking out the window too. I thought, He's afraid but he won't show it. And I thought, He doesn't know he's going to die, none of them know it. I wanted to stand up and let loose and tell them. I wanted to yell at them and smack them in their faces and I wanted to cry. It didn't seem fair that I was the only one who knew.

But I just sat there, hanging on, and I said to myself, If they don't know, they're lucky. Let it happen. At least it'll be over fast, no floating around in space the way I feared. Just one second when we hit. I can behave for that.

"Here we go," said Case.

I hung on. I thought, This is one thing I've done well. I sat back in my seat and let my hands hang loose. Once in my life and at the moment it counts, I'm a man and there's nobody to see it. It's just for me. And I thought, For once in my life I've come to terms.

The wheels hit and bounced and skidded. The pilot cut back the engines and we started taxiing to airport, racing the fire trucks back to the airport. Not a damn thing happened. It was like any landing, every landing I've ever been on, better even than some. Nothing happened. The passengers started filing out one at a time and I looked at their faces and they were just like every other landing.

I thought, It wasn't anything, it was routine, and I was the only man on this whole goddamn flight who was afraid. And so goddamn proud too. Counterfeit and phony. I could have bawled. Who isn't brave in his own head? Who can't endure something when it's nothing? How many no-deaths will I have to face? Martin Fincher, the cat with a hundred phony lives. I said to myself, Okay, buddy, face it, would you rather die than this? But then I thought, At least nobody knows about the fool but the fool himself. At least I acted right. I can't help what I feel, but I acted like everybody else.

At the foot of the stairs I waited for Case and I said, "If that pilot had just gone on to Baltimore we could have caught a better connection. Let's check the flights."

"Let's get a drink," Case said.

"Buddy," I said, "you want to go to Mississippi, you don't want to go to Mississippi? They'll have the mess cleaned up if we don't hurry."

He looked at me with a cloudy grin and he said, "Fincher, after what I've been through the last five minutes, I want a drink. The hell with Mississippi."

And I thought: I was right, he was afraid all the time. I said, "Don't tell me Jonathan Case was afraid." I just said it, didn't particularly mean to say it, just thought I'd push the advantage a little.

"Fincher, don't you have sense enough to know we almost

crashed?" he said. "Yes, I was afraid and if you want to feel so goddamn superior about it, go ahead and feel superior. I want a drink."

I wanted to hit him but I didn't. What would have been the point? A guy like me can't ever beat a guy like Case. No matter what I do, he will end up sitting on my chest. Case knows he's Case, but God knows who Martin Fincher is.

"Cheers to Jonathan Case," I said. And we went in and had a drink.

Small Moments

As the airplane lifted off the Memphis runway, Savannah Jordan looked out the porthole at the hometown she never expected to see again. She thought she identified her half-sister careening out of the parking lot in a fire-engine red Thunderbird convertible. A beautiful, tawny, enviable, guileless, slightly vulgar girl, that, and their loving father barely cold these long three weeks. Whereas, thought Savannah, I am bereft. An orphan, so to speak. At forty-two. Next to her, a young sailor yawned and, under cover of *Life* magazine, lazily scratched his crotch.

She was returning to the real world, New York, the fashion magazine she had associate edited for many years, her son, clever friends, travels. She decided to look very closely at Memphis, the river, the bluffs. Not really seeing, she imagined streets downtown leading to the water, faces, tones of Southern voices. She was touched with loss, but she was lying of course; it was only her father she mourned. Not even her mother, a lady who had drowned off St. Simon's Island while swimming with a man no one knew. Savannah's memory of her was only a memory of herself, at seven, sitting still and quiet for many minutes on her father's fat thighs, surrounded by his protecting arms, receiving his tender gaze and the news. But we have each other, perhaps he said.

Until, when Savannah was thirteen, Miss Lucy, a frail thing with beautiful pastel skin, had come to bear another three children. After that it was only a matter of time before her father would die. At eighteen she had been reluctant to go off to Sweet Briar because she expected him to succumb before the Christmas holidays. At twenty-five she wondered that he dared visit the Greek Isles for he was apt to die there, creating disturbance and inconvenience all around. She had considered postponing each of her two bad marriages to await the fatal day.

When she had first been told that he was actually dying ("failing" Miss Lucy had whispered in a haunted voice that seemed to have swept up all the ghosts along the thousand miles of wire) Savannah had felt a weight falling into place inside her.

As the plane leveled off, Savannah gazed out at the hard blue sky and the city below sinking into the red clay. She had always been mildly afraid of flying, an explosion in mid-air, falling, falling. But now in her bereavement she felt her whole being was more exposed to chance, to the elements, to the awe of death than ever before. Without thinking she spoke aloud.

"The no-smoking is off. Suppose you don't have a cigarette."

A hand holding a package of Camels came to her. She had always wondered where sailors kept their small belongings, cigarettes, wallets, prophylactics. Perhaps they wore bras.

"No thanks," she said, "I don't smoke."

A quick puzzled frown, a shrug, and the sailor dropped the package between his legs. He shifted his gaze out the window across the aisle.

That was Savannah all over, of course: yearning, remote, ironic. Exact words of her sweet dead dear old father when she had gone home for his dying. He lay in the white bed, his belly flowing down the sides of his body, his moist hand massaging hers. Don't expect so much and do expect a little more, he said. It will be worse for you each year, I hate to leave you so alone. But I'm not, not at all, she said. I'm fine. Suddenly his eyelids fluttered and his hand relaxed and she felt that she was being dragged down into the vortex of his growing darkness. She grabbed her hand away, startling him from his drifting swoon.

When the seat-belt sign went off, she thought of trying her airlegs but the thought of dragging herself, half crouching, across the sailor's lap seemed too comic. Besides, she still owed him an apology for the rebuff. She made up a nice smile to show him how friendly she was, rather than crazy, how she did take him into account, and she said, "My husband was a sailor."

"That so?" said the sailor.

"Well, no, not really. He wasn't so much a sailor as an officer and not so much a husband as an ex."

He peeked at her quickly and then moved a bit toward the aisle. "That right?"

"No, it isn't right," she said, thinking how handsome Lloyd had looked in his blues and how she had married him more for marrying than for love, and how sad and grieved her sad father had been at the divorce two years later. "It's correct but it isn't right." Because all that was gone, the blues to moths, the braid to tarnish, and her father to the fate of men. Of animals. Of vegetables. And God knows perhaps even of rocks and stars and the very waters of the earth. Oh Lord Lord.

The sailor turned toward her, now smiling, a puzzled but knowing smile. Crazy funny lady on an airplane, a good story to tell back at the boat. There was this well-dressed lady, I mean you could tell she had class.

"What boat are you on?" she asked.

"Ship?" he gently corrected her.

That had happened before. "Yes, ship ship, boats that have little boats. Having fornicated on the high seas, I guess."

His laughter lighted up his face, like peaches with fuzz on his cheeks. His belly bounced with the laughter. "I like that, that's good." He nodded his head, as if making notes. How old was he? Twenty-one maybe. A boy.

A man, she thought, is not a man until his father dies. And a woman? A clever little reversal: a woman ceases to be a woman when her father dies. Aphorisms, I love aphorisms.

She appeared at fifteen in a pale yellow ball gown and off his look of wonder and delight she caught the idea: I am a beautiful woman. Not the Southern belle, no, but something, she had been something then. A gift. I never said thanks. She stretched with a sudden feel of coldness and the sound of her breath broke coming out and she covered by saying to the sailor, "Is your father dead?"

"Why?" he asked. "What's up?" But he was game if wary, she could feel him ticking away with interest.

"Pretend I'm doing a survey."

"Yeah," he said. His face had sobered and he looked rather important. "Eight years ago."

"And are you a man?" she asked.

The boy blew air from the corner of his mouth and his belly bounced again. "Try me," he said.

"I'm sorry," she said. "I'm talking rot and I'm sorry. Okay?" She opened *Time* to "People" and pretended to read. She twisted her eyeballs to take a better look at the sailor, at the blond fuzz on his neck, at the smooth dampness of his mouth. When she cut to his eyes, his eyes had cut to hers, saying Try me, try me, and then she felt a quick soft pounding in her groin. She turned away, for she was philosophic: it's the one thing in the world that really will go away if you pretend it isn't there.

He was almost young enough to be her son. Her son was thirteen with a breaking voice and a great longing for girls. And she, surely, she now told herself, was not going to be one of those lascivious old women, soiled by using and being used, soured by their desire for the young.

She turned pages and landed at "Medicine." Hormones make all the difference. A woman could easily ride the pill into her seventies, yahooing all the way. A crew of doctors might find her a brand new heart, kidneys, somebody's liver, skin grafts, face lifts, hip shavings and breast shapings. Maybe a doctor she knew knew a virgin who was just about to die.

She was just into the forties, he was surely over twenty. She closed her eyes. She saw no harm, no carnage. Only a white field with a great white hare frolicking over it. It would do her a world of good, this one clean unambiguous moment that would proclaim that she was not in the coffin with her father. She had survived. Life affirmation and all that. And wasn't it very likely it would be fine for him too?

When she closed the magazine and pivoted on her hip, he was still saying Try me, try me, and she was answering I will, I will. She commenced to ask him questions she knew he loved: Who are you, really? What are you? What is your destiny? By the time they landed at Kennedy in mid-afternoon, she had touched his arm, his shoulder, his knee. She plied him with her wanting of him and thus she overcame the disbelief of his youth and the reticence of his ignorance, and when the engines signed off he said, "What's a woman like you doing horsing around with a guy like me?"

She would have liked five minutes in the lavatory with a make-up kit to prepare her answer. She said, in a voice of honesty, "A woman like me would like to spend the rest of the afternoon horsing around with a guy like you."

He nodded, and nodding sank a little into the collar of his uniform. It was all up to her, he couldn't quite manage it all. She arranged the props carefully, tenderly, protecting both of them. She got him to settle on a nearby airport hotel, to send her ahead in a cab. The guiding made her feel somewhat large and rawboned, assertive and unsubtle. Whistling up taxis and signing registers.

The room she engaged was a bilious green, silent and impersonal. Above the bed was a Parisian scene, yellow, pink, mauve, of a gay frivolous woman under a parasol, surrounded by young men. No hotel room was safe from that picture. This woman, this frivolous silly woman . . . was she supposed to be Savannah?

When she heard his muffled scratching at the door, she was struck by the absurdity. What failure should she accuse herself of? Taste? Sanity? Perspective? A young boy picked up on an airplane and furtively brought to this. If, she told herself, she so desperately needed that moment of affirmation, to wipe away the taste of grief, she had friends, co-workers, an old lover or two still on the edges of her life.

When she opened the door she expected to find a small tyke something less than five feet in a middy blouse, with wispy uncombable hair and chocolate stains around his lips. But the sailor had grown considerably, he quite filled the doorway. And once inside the room, he made up for his lapse of management by grabbing her and squeezing her buttocks as he kissed her.

"This is really great," he said. "I've never been with an older woman before." His smile was angelic, as simple as a baby's.

Savannah went into the bathroom, turned on the tap and listened to the water gasp. We use each other, she thought, we use each other all the time.

The sailor opened the door. He had on only his shorts which were large and flappy and his black socks which sagged to his ankle bones. He said, "Let's go, let's go," and slapped his hands together. He turned and dove over the luggage rack onto the bed and the bed cranged and heaved and he bounced on the mattress with his knees and elbows and in mid-air flipped over on his back. He held his arms toward her and she thought he came off the back row of a Botticelli and she felt again the tightening of desire.

Quite unexpectedly, she could not bear for him to see her naked, to be compared with all his youthful fineness. He was only a boy, a youth, without the kindness of age, untempered, his unfaltering gaze would take in her striated thighs, her softening bellyflesh, the shoulders grooved by bra straps.

She pressed the wall switch, and plunged the room in semidarkness. Quickly she undressed and made her way to the bed. "You look great, just great," he said, "especially when you laugh like that."

She sighed in gratitude and then put both knees on the bed. As she dropped toward him, she said, "I think I'll invent a science of reading character through belly buttons." Her face fell forward to explore this very sweet and simple character with whom she would embark on this very simple act.

At early twilight they woke together, face to face. The sailor looked, at first, questioning and doubtful, a how-was-I look. She scrubbed his nose with her fingernail, rubbing off the pale freckles, tenderly maternal. She had had her moment of affirmation, had gotten what she wanted, gotten what she usually got within a usual variation. Was, of course, disappointed. Wanted to apologize for her disappointment, wanted to tell him there was nothing personal in it. Nothing personal!

"Was it good?" asked the sailor in a voice that reproved her for not volunteering.

"Marvelous," she said. It lacked conviction, and he deserved conviction. "If it weren't so darn late, or tomorrow if only you didn't have to report . . ." The sailor relaxed, quite contented, she thought, not to perform again, not go through the anxiety of performing for an experienced, self-contained middle-aged woman who God knows what she did expect. Poor dear. Savannah laughed.

He said, "You know you're really a funny one."

"I have my moments," she said.

While they dressed the sailor shot her odd, appealing, increasingly uneasy and resentful glances. She wanted to help him but what could she say? That she had expected, under the circumstances, failure or fantastic bliss? intensification or diminution? that whatever it was, it was her business, not his? He would never understand that. She went on fastening her stockings to supporters that dangled from her girdle. She could at least offer him that.

The boy got into his uniform. Straightening suddenly and with a look that was sullen and suspicious, he said, "I didn't do a damn thing for you, did I? Maybe when women get to your age . . ."

She heard the echo, You are ugly, you are old. But of course she was, wasn't that the point? But she owed him more than the truth. She dredged up for him the most dazzling smile she could find in an old mildewed steamer trunk of other days filled with dazzling smiles of ecstasy and gratitude and fine humor.

"No," she said. "Don't ruin it, you were so wonderful."

He said, "Shut up" but his face said he believed her and forgave her. He put his hat on and jerked it down on both sides and with springing steps walked to the door. "Thanks a bunch, I enjoyed it."

The door slammed behind him. Savannah looked carefully at the picture above the rumpled bed. She imagined her own aging face beneath the parasol. She saw herself prancing along the paths in the parks of the world's great cities, gay, flirtatious, alert, seeking in young strangers those large heavy-lidded eyes, the fat gentle hands, the heavy fat body that had shielded her from ugliness and age. She held back from giving herself fully to this vision, for great gestures eluded her.